"You can't just go around kissing people!"

Erin took a deep breath and continued. "Look, I don't need this kind of aggravation from you. You're already causing enough problems in my life."

"Aggravation . . . so that's what it's called." Will's tone was solemn as he fingered a curl of her hair, but Erin sensed his amusement.

Joining in the spirit of conviviality, Will's ridiculous dog, Duffy, sat on her foot. Will curled another strand of her hair around his finger. Erin decided that the entire Kendrick clan was getting a little too chummy. "Look, let's get down to business—"

"That's what we're doing."

Erin froze. There was no longer any doubt about it. She was being cleverly bamboozled by Will Kendrick and his untidy mop of a Scottie!

Ellen James has wanted a writing career ever since she won a national short-story contest when she was in high school. *Love's Harbor* is her fourth Harlequin Romance novel, and readers will be interested to note that the hero's dog, Duffy, was modeled on Ellen's own Scottie—Duffy. She and her husband, both writers, love to travel and share an interest in wildlife photography and American history.

Books by Ellen James

HARLEQUIN ROMANCE

LOVE'S HARBOR
Ellen James

Harlequin Books

TORONTO • NEW YORK • LONDON
AMSTERDAM • PARIS • SYDNEY • HAMBURG
STOCKHOLM • ATHENS • TOKYO • MILAN

ISBN 0-373-03154-8

Harlequin Romance first edition October 1991

LOVE'S HARBOR

CHAPTER ONE

"WHAT DO YOU KNOW—the blasted rumors are true, after all. You're Ned Lewis's niece, barging into town just like everyone said. Lord, you even look the same as your uncle. It's like seeing Ned rise from the grave to plague me all over again. I'm living my own worst nightmare!"

These words were not exactly welcoming. They were hardly flattering, either. Erin pushed back a wisp of her bright red hair and stared at the man who had appeared so abruptly in the doorway to Uncle Ned's office. Actually, it was her office now. She had to keep reminding herself of that fact.

"Yes...Ned was my uncle. I'm Erin Lewis. Can I help you?" she asked in a calm, controlled voice. She'd been in the newspaper business long enough to learn that keeping her volatile temper in check was usually the wisest policy. This man, however, was already taxing her best efforts at self-restraint. He prowled into her office like a cantankerous leopard and slapped both hands on her desk. He bent down and glared straight into her face.

"Same carroty hair," he muttered. "Same blue eyes and stubborn nose as old Ned. How can that be? One Ned Lewis was more than enough for Cape Cod."

Erin sat up straighter in Uncle Ned's battered and torn leather chair. She pressed her own hands down on the scarred surface of the desk. She'd turned twenty-seven last month, and certainly at this stage in her life she didn't have to tolerate insults about the color of her hair. As a kid she'd suffered enough with the nicknames "Big Red" and "Carrot Brain." Her only consolation had been knowing that she looked so much like her wonderful Uncle Ned.

Now she coolly assessed the stranger in front of her, wondering how he had acquired such an irrational dislike for her uncle. The man had unruly black hair that looked as if it had been tousled by a strong sea breeze. His eyes were a deep brown, his features rough-hewn and irregular. He was wearing a shirt so worn and faded it was impossible to tell what the original color had been. Under the threadbare cloth, however, a powerfully built torso was very much in evidence.

Erin shifted uneasily in her chair, trying to edge farther away from the man. Suddenly she was too aware of his virility, his vibrancy. He looked like a husky fisherman who had just sailed his boat into harbor with the fleet. Only he didn't smell anything like cod or mackerel. Erin found herself sniffing the air appreciatively. He had brought with him the tang of salt air on a summer day and the clean scent of sun-bleached cotton.

Goodness, couldn't she keep her own olfactory glands under control? "Obviously you had some sort of grudge against my uncle. But I'm sure we can straighten out any misunderstandings. Why don't you have a seat and we'll talk about this from the beginning?"

The man leaned closer to her in a menacing fashion. "Enough talk has gone on already in this office. That's all Ned Lewis ever did—blather away at anyone fool enough to listen."

By now Erin had crammed her chair clean up against the wall, trying to maintain some distance between herself and this stranger. She scowled back at him. "It's true that my uncle had a special way with words. That's why he was such a good writer—such a good newspaperman."

"Hah!" That one syllable was loaded with scorn. "The *Cape Cod Gazette* has been a joke for years. Old Ned didn't know a thing about running a newspaper."

Anger flashed through Erin. She struggled up from the big chair and marched around the desk to the far wall. She gestured at the plaques hanging there. "'Ned Lewis, Journalist of the Year,'" she read out loud. "'To Edward H. Lewis, in honor of editorial excellence.' As you can see, not everyone shared your opinion about my uncle, Mr.—whoever you are."

He didn't bother to introduce himself, but he did come over to examine the tarnished plaques. "Look at the dates on these. The most recent one is over thirty years ago. That tells the whole story about Ned Lewis. He didn't do one constructive thing the last three decades of his life. Unless you count sweet-talking gullible women out of their money."

Erin clenched her fists. When she spoke, her voice was glacier-cold. "You've just made a serious accusation against my uncle. I think you'd better explain it or retract it."

The man surprised her with a slow grin. "Well, I'll say this much for you, Ms. Erin Lewis. You didn't inherit any of your uncle's infamous talent for speechifying. You get right to the point. That's to your credit, believe me."

The man had goaded her too far, and Erin's control snapped. Maybe she wasn't known for her eloquent speech, but she was famous enough for her temper. She felt her face heating up and knew it was probably turning as red as her hair.

"Who the hell are you?" she bellowed. "And just what the hell do you want?"

His smile turned grim. "I'm Will Kendrick. My aunt is Margaret Kendrick, a very well-meaning but naive woman who signed over her entire life's savings to your Uncle Ned. What do I want? I want to get my aunt's money back, that's what I want. And even if I have to shut down this sorry excuse for a newspaper, that's what I'll do!"

He knew how to give a pretty good bellow himself. But Erin couldn't believe what he was telling her. She almost laughed.

"Uncle Ned would never have taken someone's money. He was too proud—too determined to make his own way in life. That's why the *Cape Cod Gazette* was never a financial success. He just wouldn't accept any help. But I'm going to turn the newspaper around. You're not going to shut it down and neither is anyone else." She spoke with conviction, shoving back a few stray curls of her hair. Then she faced Will

Kendrick squarely. She was tall, but she had to tilt her head back to glare up at him. Erin didn't like that. As a newspaper reporter she'd learned to take advantage of her height. She preferred to confront men at her own level; a shorter man was even better. And when necessary, she was very good at delivering an intimidating stare.

Will Kendrick, however, wasn't showing any signs that he felt intimidated by her. In fact, he was looking at her with an expression that seemed disturbingly like pity. "Old Ned duped you better than anyone else, it seems. His own niece, at that."

"I knew my uncle very well—"

"How well, Erin?" When he spoke her name, the sound was far too intimate, as if he were savoring the syllables on his tongue. His unexpected gentleness put her off-balance; she wished he'd go back to yelling. Then she could do some satisfying yelling in return.

She went to the window and gazed out toward Cape Cod Bay. Memories of her childhood sparkled in her mind like sunshine on water. "When I was a kid, I used to come here every summer and help Uncle Ned with the newspaper. He treated me as an equal—the two of us confided in each other. I knew him very well, Mr. Kendrick. And I'll stake everything on his integrity."

"Summers...now I remember. There used to be a hot-tempered little redheaded kid always hanging out around the wharves. So that was you. And here you are now, more of a fiery redhead than ever."

She swiveled around toward him. "I hate it when people call me that! 'Fiery redhead,' indeed. I mean, they take one look at the color of my hair and assume I have a hot temper to go along with it. Just like that. It's infuriating. It's—'' She stopped, listening to Will Kendrick as he chuckled at her. He had a good chuckle, deep in tone but comfortable and easy on the ear. Erin was annoyed with herself for liking the sound of it so much. She folded her arms against her chest.

"All right," she admitted grudgingly. "Maybe I am a little . . . combustible. But can you imagine what it's like, constantly hearing that you're a spitfire or a red-quilled porcupine? When I was a kid it was even worse. They called me Matchstick back then." Erin clamped her mouth shut, appalled at what she'd just said. She had let slip the most dreadful nickname of her childhood: Matchstick. None of the other nick-names she'd been cursed with in her life could possibly equal the humiliation of that particular one!

Erin swung around behind her desk again. She reached into the top drawer and extracted a notepad. Plunking herself down in the tattered leather chair, she uncapped a pen. "Very well, Mr. Kendrick. Let's get down to business, shall we? I want to know the truth about this alleged aunt of yours and her so-called life savings. Have a seat over there, please."

He remained standing, watching her with a be-mused expression. Unfortunately she was quick to blush and her face started heating up again. She could feel her earlobes tingling under Will Kendrick's scru-tiny. But at last he went over to the old-fashioned wooden office chair she'd indicated for him. He set-tled down in it and casually brought his leg up to rest an ankle on his knee. The faded denim of his jeans stretched across a muscular thigh. His foot jiggled up and down as if in rhythm to some unheard beat. He was wearing scuffed running shoes with the heels worn down almost to nonexistence. Apparently Will Kendrick wasn't a man who liked to discard any item of clothing, no matter how well used.

"I've already told you the truth," he said. "Your uncle was full of schemes for expanding the newspaper, even though he could never pay his bills. He convinced Aunt Maggie that great days were ahead for the *Cape Cod Gazette.* She thought she was making an investment. Unfortunately it was only after Ned died that I discovered she'd cleaned out her savings account for him. And then I found out *you* were coming to town, with some damn fool idea about running the newspaper yourself."

Erin jotted down the name "Aunt Maggie" on her yellow pad, followed by the words "obnoxious nephew." Then she glanced up. "The *Gazette* is my inheritance. Uncle Ned left the paper to me, so of course I'm going to run it. He trusted me to do just that, and I'm not going to let him down."

Will's foot jiggled with a little more force. "You don't seem to be listening to me. Maggie didn't hand over just a few bucks to your uncle. We're talking about a hundred thousand dollars here."

Erin drew in her breath. The pen fell from her fingers and rolled about unheeded on the desk. "Why would Uncle Ned take that much money from someone? It doesn't make any sense! Whenever my parents tried to offer him a loan, he refused. He said there was no way his younger brother was going to support him. Now I'm supposed to believe he'd accept a small fortune from some innocent elderly lady?''

"Maggie's hardly an elderly woman," Will remarked in a dry tone. "She's only sixty, and she looks ten years younger than that. She was Ned's... girlfriend, I guess you could say." He seemed disgusted with the idea. Erin herself was surprised.

"This is sounding more and more odd to me all the time. Uncle Ned didn't say anything in his letters about a special woman. In fact, he was quite shy with women. That's why he never married."

Will stared at her with an expression of incredulity. "You're dead wrong about that. Ned Lewis liked having a reputation as a ladies' man. He had affairs all over Cape Cod, and prided himself on every one of them."

Erin gripped her pen again, wanting to hurl it at Will. But it would make an ineffectual weapon against the wretched lies he was telling her. "Look, Mr. Kendrick," she said, her voice shaking with anger now. "I don't know what your real purpose is in all this. Maybe Uncle Ned wrote a news story you didn't like. So you thought up some sick joke and came barreling in here, trying to destroy his reputation—"

"Lord, you really worshiped the old guy, didn't you?"

Will's question cut straight through to the heart of her feelings for Uncle Ned. But Ned had deserved every bit of her high regard. It seemed important to convince Will Kendrick of this one fact. She propped her elbows on the desk.

"Listen, my uncle was someone very special to me. There were plenty of reasons for that, you know. He taught me so many things, after my own parents had practically given up on me. They told me I was incorrigible. But Ned told me I was spunky, and that made all the difference in how I looked at myself." Erin smiled gently as she remembered. "He was an idealistic person, always ready to see the best in me. But that meant he also demanded the best. He gave me both discipline and love when I was growing up. Ned Lewis was just someone…exceptional. And you know what? I've never yet encountered a man who could measure up to him." Erin gazed pointedly at Will, to convey her belief that *he* didn't measure up to Uncle Ned in any way.

Will only shook his head. "I feel sorry for you, Erin. Apparently you never really knew your uncle at all. You're in for a lot of disillusionment, I'm afraid. But that can't be helped. And somehow you're going to have to find a way to pay back Maggie's money."

Erin drew a jagged dollar sign on her notepad. "Where's the proof of your allegations? You haven't shown me any loan agreement between Ned and this Aunt Maggie of yours. And no one challenged his will, that's another thing."

"Believe me, I would have contested the damn will if I'd known about Maggie's savings in time. Maggie trusted your uncle, that's the problem. She never asked him to sign his name to anything. Just handed over all that money to him! Besides, do you actually think old Ned would've compromised himself in writing, unless he'd been forced into it?"

Erin drew another line on her pad, this one so emphatic that the pen almost ripped through the paper. "I want to speak to your aunt. I need to hear her version of the story."

Will remained seated in the same casual pose as before, but his muscles seemed to tense. "You're not going to bother Maggie with this. She's been through enough because of Ned Lewis, and I don't want her dragged into anything else. You'll have to deal directly with me. I'm representing my aunt."

Erin looked him over skeptically. "What are you, some kind of lawyer?"

He smiled at her with unconvincing geniality. "I run a boat yard. If you ever want to take up sailing, I'm the man to see."

Erin smacked her notepad facedown on the desk. "Mr. Kendrick, I find it very suspicious that you don't want me to speak with your aunt. And you haven't given me any tangible proof of your story. It's been nothing but accusations."

"I'll tell you what's tangible. Maggie saving up her alimony checks year after year. Never wasting a penny of her money until Ned Lewis started filling her head with garbage about the wonderful future of the *Cape Cod Gazette*. But I'll tell you something else, Erin. I'm a reasonable person. I'm willing to negotiate on this."

He sounded anything but reasonable, and Erin didn't trust him. "Suppose I did believe you—exactly what is your idea of negotiation?"

Will stretched out both his legs and clasped his hands over his stomach. He actually seemed to be enjoying himself. "Well, now, something tells me you don't have an extra hundred thousand just lying around." He glanced about the office with its shabby wood paneling and cobwebbed ceiling. "Most likely you'll have to liquidate the newspaper," he mused, "which means Jamesport will finally be rid of the *Cape Cod Gazette.* You'll be performing a public service. Sure, you won't get much money out of the sale, but it should be enough to start making payments to my aunt. You see how fair I'm being? I'm not asking you to pay her back all at once."

Erin gouged her pen into one of the many nicks on the desktop. "What you're proposing is impossible! I can't sell the *Gazette.* It was Uncle Ned's whole life. He counted on me to keep it running, and I'm not going to disappoint him."

Will Kendrick's dark brown eyes held no warmth or sympathy for her. "I can always take this to court, Erin, if you refuse to cooperate with me. Aunt Maggie doesn't have anyone else to look after her interests. I'm not going to let *her* down. Your uncle's already dead. But Maggie's alive and she has a lot of years left to her. Seems to me that gives her a few extra rights in this whole mess."

To her own fury, Erin couldn't think of a single argument against his. If he was telling the truth, something would have to be done about this Maggie Kendrick. Surely Uncle Ned would have had a good reason to borrow that much money from her; at the same time, he wouldn't have wanted her to go destitute.

Will stood up, lithe and easy in his movements. He leaned over her desk again. This time she didn't seem able to move away from him but found herself gazing at his strong, expressive mouth.

"Too bad you're Ned Lewis's niece," he remarked. "Otherwise I think you and I could enjoy getting to know each other. Don't you agree, Erin?" There was laughter in his voice. He was taunting her, damn it, and she couldn't think of one decent retort. She was too mesmerized by this close-up view of his eyes. From this vantage point, a golden light seemed to shimmer under the deep brown of his irises.

He straightened up and walked to the door. "I'll be seeing you, Erin. Something tells me we're going to work this out just fine." He sounded completely sure of himself, as if he didn't consider her a threatening opponent in the least.

"No one is going to take away this newspaper!" she declared.

He gave her an unperturbed grin, then disappeared through the doorway as suddenly as he had come.

Erin dug her nails into the palms of her hands. She scrunched her eyes shut. "One hundred, ninety-nine, ninety-eight . . ." She counted slowly and deliberately, using the method Uncle Ned had taught her for cooling down when she was flaming mad like this. It had been a long time since anyone had destroyed her composure so thoroughly. She'd learned, with a great deal of pain and difficulty, how to keep her mercurial temperament subdued. And she'd finally reached a point where only occasionally did she succumb to an outburst of emotion. Yet one encounter with Will Kendrick had disrupted years of self-discipline.

"Sixty-two, sixty-one, sixty..." She was still simmering. More than anything, she was angry at herself for being attracted to Will. In fact, she was very attracted to him. What was wrong with her? He was threatening to take away the *Gazette,* and all she could think about was the way his hair curled behind his ears. For goodness' sake, Will Kendrick wasn't even her type of man! Not at all.

"Thirty-nine, thirty-eight," she proclaimed loudly, tapping her heels against the wooden floor for extra emphasis. Usually she was calm by the time she counted down to sixty-five. Today, however, the counting method wasn't helping one bit. "Oh, confoundation!" What she really needed was a plan of action. She had to start fighting Will Kendrick right away.

First of all, she needed to know the truth. Had Uncle Ned, in fact, taken all that money from Margaret Kendrick? Erin started yanking open desk drawers, searching for Ned's ledger book. All his papers were in a jumble—scribbled notes for news stories that had gone to press years ago, crumpled receipts, empty candy-bar wrappers, letters that were yellowed with age. The ledger was buried at the bottom of one drawer, and Erin hauled it out. Opening it on the desk, she scanned the latest entries. There was only one problem. It appeared that Ned had stopped doing his books some ten years ago. The latest figure jotted down was a disbursement for repairs to the cantankerous old printing press...dated about the same time Erin had graduated from high school.

She grimaced and began rummaging through the desk drawers again. This time she found a better prize—Ned's big, unwieldy checkbook. Flipping through it, she discovered that he'd written out a surprising number of checks in the few months before his death. Most of them seemed to be payments to his creditors—the newsprint supplier, a roofing-repair company, more servicemen come to tinker with the old press. There were also check stubs made out to several individuals in town: Hannibal S. Greene, Ulysses Baird, Thomas Parnell. On the last stub was scribbled, "Finally paid back these bozos!" Altogether, the checks added up to an alarming sum of money. It was obvious that Ned had recently come into some healthy funds.

Erin rubbed her temples, trying to decide which course to take next. She was still mourning for her Uncle Ned. His death from a heart attack had been so sudden—so unfair. Erin hadn't even been able to attend his funeral, having to remain in Chicago to cover an important news story. She'd felt guilty about that, although Uncle Ned would have understood. He had been proud of her for landing such a good job as a reporter for a major Chicago paper. And it had been his dream that one day she would take over the *Cape Cod Gazette*.

No one in Erin's family seemed able to understand that Ned's dream was also her own. When she'd announced her decision to move to Cape Cod, her family had been truly perplexed—wondering why on earth Erin wanted to leave a comfortable, secure job to run a struggling little newspaper.

Erin hadn't known how to answer. She'd merely surveyed her family in silence: her mother, her father and her two sisters, all four of them possessing sober brown hair and even tempers. Somehow Erin had popped up among these placid people, starting out as a squalling redheaded baby who had given her mother no end of grief. People had often asked if Erin was adopted, and as she grew she wondered about that possibility herself. But then one summer, when she was an unmanageable eight-year-old, her parents had sent her off in desperation to Ned Lewis on Cape Cod. Uncle Ned, with bright red hair the exact same shade as hers. From the first moment she'd looked into his shrewd and kind blue eyes—eyes so like her own— she'd realized that she truly did belong with someone. And even though Uncle Ned had died, she still belonged.

Somehow she had to save his newspaper. She owed at least that much to him—and she owed it to herself, too. Her job as a newspaper reporter in Chicago had been challenging and fulfilling, but now Erin had a chance to be her own boss. Like Ned, she cherished the freedom of running her own small paper. Will Kendrick wasn't going to snatch that away from her before she'd even had a chance to get started! She'd find a way to resolve this problem.

She pushed back her chair and walked quickly through the hallway of the cavernous newspaper building. The place was much too quiet now, Ned's few employees long gone to more lucrative jobs elsewhere. But Erin was accompanied by her memories. On her left was the composing room, where the ancient Linotype machine had performed faithfully over the years. Deeper still in the building was the room where the cranky printing press held court. Uncle Ned had often joked that the press was just like Erin herself—temperamental and willful, but always coming through in the end. She could almost hear his voice booming out at her from the shadows: "Spirit, Erin! That's what you and that grand old machine have in common. Don't you ever forget it, girl. Spirit will pull the two of you through every time."

The memory heartened her. She lifted her chin a little higher, straightening her shoulders into the posture that emphasized rather than diminished her height. She went up the narrow staircase that led to Uncle Ned's living quarters on the second floor. This was now to be her own apartment, but everywhere she looked were the remnants of Ned's life. Littering the floor were cardboard boxes buckling with the weight of books; stacks of the *Cape Cod Gazette* that had never sold were scattered about here and there; old maps were rolled up in the corners or tacked to the walls. Erin would have to sort out all the clutter and begin to create her own home here. It would be difficult to throw anything away, for Ned had accumulated each item with some future adventure in mind. He'd started collecting maps to document his trips around the world...trips that had somehow never materialized.

Erin tried to shake off her regret for the lost opportunities in Ned's life. What she needed to do was concentrate on revitalizing his legacy. Perhaps she was encountering more opposition than she'd expected, but that wasn't going to stop her! She knew what she had to do next, regardless of Will Kendrick's wishes.

In the bedroom she grabbed up her navy blue felt hat and crammed it low over her forehead. She gave herself a glance in the mirror. Red curls tumbled down to her shoulders from under the hat. Long ago she'd given up trying to tame her hair and now allowed it to be as wild and exuberant as it pleased. She'd learned to be grateful for its thick, luxuriant texture. And she was almost resigned to the fate of possessing skin that flushed so easily and betrayed all her emotions. On the occasions when her skin wasn't glowing a bright pink, it had a pure, creamy tone she'd come to appreciate.

Erin examined her face dispassionately in the mirror—wide-spaced blue eyes, a nose that was most definite about taking its place, a mouth that was broad and full, a jaw that was strongly molded. Well, she was comfortable with her looks and that was enough. This was yet another lesson Uncle Ned had taught her when she was a teenager and despaired of ever overcoming her own gawkiness. He'd shown her how to stand up straight instead of hunching her shoulders, how to toss back her wild mass of curls and stare everyone straight in the eye. She owed so much to him!

"I'm not going to let you down, Uncle Ned," she whispered to the dusty, untidy rooms around her. "You can count on that—I won't disappoint you." Then she clattered back down the stairs, ready to do battle in Jamesport, Cape Cod.

CHAPTER TWO

THE HOUSE WAS SNUG and trim, a traditional Cape Cod saltbox with a long sloping roof in back and two even rows of windows in front. It was painted a cheerful apple-green, with shining white trim all around. According to the telephone book, this was where Margaret Kendrick lived...Will Kendrick's Aunt Maggie.

Erin went up the brick walkway and lifted the brass knocker on the door. She assumed someone was at home, for there was a car in the drive. It was a little 1950s Metropolitan in superb condition, all pink-and-white curves. Was Aunt Maggie a connoisseur of vintage cars? Or maybe she was one of those people who bought a vehicle and then simply couldn't bear to part with it, even after thirty or forty years.

No one came to the door after several knocks, but Erin thought she saw one of the upstairs curtains twitch. She frowned and gave an extra-hard rap on the door, using her knuckles this time instead of the knocker. But still no one came in response. Erin surveyed the little garden in front of the house. All the flower beds were carefully tended, the roses and larkspur flourishing. Maggie Kendrick lived in cozy but simple surroundings. She obviously wasn't rich, and the sum of one hundred thousand dollars probably meant a great deal to her. Erin hoped fervently that Will's story wasn't true—in spite of the evidence she'd found in Uncle Ned's checkbook. She gave one last look around, then walked back down the brick pathway. If Maggie Kendrick wouldn't speak to her, she'd have to try someone else.

Only a short while later Erin was seated in the office of Harold Fiske. Mr. Fiske was an overly cheerful man who had been Uncle Ned's banker in Jamesport.

"Yes, yes, good old Ned," chortled Mr. Fiske, reclining in his chair and pulling on the blind cord at the window. The blind shot upward and summer sunshine splashed into the room. "At one time or another, Ned owed money to practically everyone in town, Miss Lewis. Not to mention the fact that he was considerably past due on his mortgage payments. I was about to foreclose on him." Mr. Fiske chuckled as if he'd made a particularly funny joke. His smooth, bald head gleamed in the sun. Then he pulled on the cord again and the blind came rattling down to cover the window.

Erin blinked, trying to adjust her eyes to these rapid changes in light. "And that's when Uncle Ned came so unexpectedly into a large amount of money?"

"Tell you what happened, Miss Lewis. About a month before he died, Ned sashayed in here grinning like he'd just robbed a bank." Mr. Fiske laughed at his own wit. "Oh, my... anyway, Ned seemed mighty pleased with himself that day. Said he'd found the solution to all his money problems, and I wasn't to bother him any more with past-due statements." Mr. Fiske paused at this crucial point in his narrative, fingering the blind cord. Erin scooted to the edge of her chair, gazing at him expectantly.

"Well?" she prodded.

ZING! The blind went shooting up again, and at the same time a hearty guffaw erupted from Mr. Fiske. "Crazy old Ned! He came right into this office here and tossed down a bundle of cash on my desk. Mighty big bundle it was, too—nothing but ten-dollar bills. He always did like to make a production out of everything. 'I'm paying off my mortgage,' he says, and he throws down all those bills. 'Matter of fact, I'm paying off everyone. Now don't go hounding me anymore,' he says, and he walks right back out again. That old coot—begging your pardon, Miss Lewis. It's bad luck to speak ill of the dead, you know." Mr. Fiske actually looked solemn for a moment, and he glanced around as if expecting to see Ned's ghost in his office.

Erin leaned forward, intent on learning one thing. "Did my uncle's sudden change of fortune have anything to do with a woman named Margaret Kendrick?"

The blind inched downward, Mr. Fiske playing with the cord as if it were a kite string. "I don't think I should discuss this," he said in a doubtful voice. "Margaret is, after all, one of our clients also..." However, Mr. Fiske's relish for gossip overcame his reticence. At last he gave another chuckle, although this one was somewhat restrained. "Ned and Maggie were an item, all right. Looked like things were getting serious between them. That was unusual for Ned—he didn't like his women to start having expectations, if you know what I mean. But I guess money always helps to ease the pain." Mr. Fiske snickered in an unsavory manner. "Ned was pretty sly about the whole thing. He had Maggie withdraw her savings in stages, so even I didn't think to question her. Then he starts paying off all his debts and talking about the new days ahead for the *Cape Cod Gazette*."

Erin sat in rigid silence, but her stomach was roiling. She felt as if she'd betrayed Uncle Ned by listening to this miserable account. Unfortunately it only confirmed what Will Kendrick had already told her. She made a few rough calculations in her head. All those checks Uncle Ned had written out, plus a lump sum in cash to pay off the mortgage on the newspaper building...yes, that was close enough to one hundred thousand dollars. Erin winced. She'd come here for information, but now she was sorry she had.

She rose from her chair and stared at Mr. Fiske. He was beginning to look apologetic, yet nothing seemed capable of entirely destroying his good humor. He fiddled with the blind cord, getting ready for another go with it.

"Now, about your own banking needs, Miss Lewis..."

"I don't need anything further from you, Mr. Fiske," she cut in with distaste. "I'll have no dealings with you in the future. You're right—you shouldn't talk about your clients." She turned and strode from the room, but not before she heard that confounded blind go screeching upward again.

Outside, the narrow streets were crowded with people in shorts and T-shirts, ready to have fun on a beautiful New England afternoon. Erin jostled her way among them, yet she felt as lonely as if she were walking by herself. How could she believe that Uncle Ned had been an opportunist and a womanizer? Nowhere in her memories of him could she find any validation for such an image. She'd spent every summer vacation with him from the time she was eight years old. Even after she went away to college and took the job in Chicago, Ned had stayed in close touch with her. They'd talked often by phone and she had a whole packet of his letters. Darn it, she'd *known* him! He'd been a kind, warm and generous man.

Erin was angry at the tears that burned behind her eyelids. Blubbering wasn't going to be of any use to her. She had to call upon all her skills as a journalist so she could discover the unbiased truth about this story. Will Kendrick was the actual source of her problems at the moment, so she'd focus on him. When looking for Maggie's address, she'd scanned the phone book for the location of Will's business. Now she headed purposefully along the waterfront.

Kendrick's Boat Yard wasn't difficult to find. It had its own pier and a tackle shop housed in a small wooden building. Erin went into the shop and found herself surrounded by an intriguing jumble of fishing rods, reels, hooks, nets and bait boxes. Behind the counter sat an elderly grizzled man who was flipping through a sports magazine. He looked Erin over as if surveying his latest catch of bluefish. Then he went back to his magazine.

"You're that niece of old Ned's," he said in a raspy voice as he studied a picture of two hockey players going after each other with their sticks. Erin thrummed her fingers on the countertop. She was getting pretty tired of hearing her uncle referred to as "old Ned" in a condescending tone that suggested he'd been some pathetic laughable creature. Why, this man sitting in front of her was probably ten years older than Ned had been at the time of his death. Certainly he didn't possess any of Ned's vigor or dynamic enthusiasm. So who was he to talk?

Erin frowned at him. "I'd like to speak to Will Kendrick. Where is he?"

The man didn't answer Erin at all, behaving as if she were no more significant than one of the fishing rods propped along the wall.

"Excuse me. Could you *please* tell me where Will Kendrick is?"

The old man turned another page of his magazine and at the same time jabbed one of his knobby fingers in the direction of the door. "On the dock," he said, offering no further help.

Erin went to the door. She glanced back at the man hunched behind the counter; he was like a gnarled root that had been growing there for ages. Kendrick's Boat Yard could certainly use a little improvement in the customer-service department, no doubt about that. Anyone would be better than this nasty old man.

"Haven't ever seen William this riled up about a woman," the man suddenly remarked to her. "You got him goin' something fierce. If I was you, missie, I'd just turn around and scuttle on home again. You don't want to be around William when he's in a snarl like this.''

Erin looked sharply at the man. She thought she detected a suspicious glint of humor in his rheumy gray eyes, but it was hard to tell. ''Humph!'' was the only response she had to offer to his warning. If Will Kendrick was spoiling for a fight, then so was she. **Erin** pushed her way out through the door.

Beyond the tackle shop was a big warehouse-type building that also seemed to be part of the boat yard. But Erin concentrated her attention on the pier, stepping onto the wooden planks. On either side of her, boats of different sizes, shapes and colors rocked gently at their moorings. Will Kendrick was nowhere in sight, and Erin walked farther along the pier. She went all the way to the end and turned back again. Now she saw a stocky black dog trotting toward her. Actually it looked more like a walking rug than a dog. It stopped a few feet away from her, black eyes peering out from under a tangle of hair. There was so much hair, in fact, that it was impossible to tell what the dog's mood might be. Menacing...simply curious? Erin didn't have a great deal of experience with four-footed species of any type; her life had been spent chasing down news stories on the two-footed variety of animal. She maintained a wary stance, hoping the dog didn't decide to charge her. It had a hefty snout for being so short and stubby.

But then, after a moment, its tail waved like a flag. Erin bent down and held out her hand, which was thoroughly sniffed over by a big friendly nose. She felt she was being given a special invitation to pet the dog between its pointy ears. She proceeded to do just that.

"Say, you're a Scottish terrier, aren't you?" she murmured. "Except that no one would know it under that mop of fur you have. I think you're due for a serious haircut."

As she uttered this statement, Will emerged from the cabin of a sailboat nearby. His expression was ominous. "Wait just a minute, Lewis. No one's going to take any shears to my dog. Get that idea right out of your head."

She straightened up. "But the poor dog needs to be groomed. Look at how it's panting! All that hair is disturbing its temperature balance. Why, any minute now it could overheat and keel over—just like that."

Will pushed back the brim of his shapeless, faded cap. "Lord, you talk about him like he's a household appliance. But he's not an 'it.' His name is Duffy, and he's just fine the way he is. His life is set up exactly how he likes it. For one thing, he hates going to the groomer's, and he knows I'll always respect that."

Erin shook her head in disapproval. "If he was my dog, he'd be under the scissors so fast he wouldn't know what hit him."

In spite of this brutal statement, Duffy obligingly wagged his tail and moved a little closer to her. He settled down and started licking his paws, as if he thought he was a cat.

Will rubbed his jaw as he regarded the dog. "He seems to like you, Erin. That's odd. Duffy's always had good judgment about people before this." He made it sound as if Duffy's powers of discernment were not to be trusted where Erin was concerned. But she herself felt honored by the Scottie's ready approval of her.

"Duffy knows I'm not someone to be underestimated," she declared.

Will turned from studying the dog to give her a frank inspection. Standing down there in the boat, he seemed to have a particularly advantageous view of her legs. Erin felt her knees tingle. Oh, for pity's sake, was it possible that even her kneecaps were going to blush now? She didn't care at all for the unsettling physical effect Will Kendrick had on her. And she didn't care for the lazy grin transforming his face. Darn, he *was* attractive.

"You look like you just stepped out of a 1940s movie," he said, his grin widening. She didn't know whether or not he meant this as a compliment, and she angled her hat more severely over her forehead. It was because of hats that Erin's particular style had developed in the first place. Her skin was so fair and prone to burn that she always had to protect it from the sun. She'd learned that a person didn't have to make do with ordinary head coverings—not when there were fedoras, straw boaters and floppy-brimmed cloches to choose from. And once you started wearing hats, other things were sure to follow…low-waisted dresses reminiscent of the 1920s, gray-flannel suits with padded shoulders, open-toed pumps, long white gloves to the elbow. It was very difficult not to get carried away.

Now Erin smoothed the waist of her tailored skirt that could easily have been in style some fifty years ago. "We need to talk, Mr. Kendrick. About this matter of your aunt's money—"

"Might as well call me Will from now on. Jump aboard and we'll talk."

Erin surveyed the sailboat. "I'd prefer a more businesslike atmosphere. Don't you have an office we can use?"

Will started coiling up some ropes. "Ever since I was a kid, I promised myself I'd never work in an office. So I sure don't have one now. Besides, Duffy and I are just about to take off for an afternoon of sailing. Come on, boy! Time to go."

Duffy perked up his ears and scrambled to attention. The next thing Erin knew, the dog was flying through the air like a woolly cannonball. He landed with a "plunk!" in the middle of the boat.

"Your turn next, Erin," Will said.

"This is ridiculous. I need to have a serious discussion with you. And I don't have a lot of time to waste."

"We'll discuss anything you like...once we're out in the bay. Besides, sailing is never a waste of time. As a matter of fact, it's what life is all about. Haven't you discovered that yet?" He sounded completely serious. Erin gazed down at him, for a moment feeling oddly off-balance. It was as if the boards under her feet had suddenly shifted. She stepped back a little, but even so she couldn't stop herself from looking into the rich brown depths of his eyes.

"Are you coming or not?" He stood there in the boat, feet spread apart, looking as sturdy and immovable as the mast that rose above him. It was obvious from his stubborn expression that he wasn't going to budge.

"If the mountain won't come to you, then you just have to go to the darn mountain yourself," she muttered.

"What was that?"

"Nothing. Just hold your ship steady, will you? Here I come." She strode forward briskly and hopped onto the edge of the boat.

"Lord, never board on the gunwale," Will yelled at her. She couldn't argue with him because she was rocking wildly on her perch as the boat listed to one side. The smooth soles of her shoes began to slip, and in another second she'd be splashing into the water!

Will grasped her around the waist and lifted her down to safety beside him. She ended up cradled against his chest, caught in the warm embrace of his arms. But there was nothing warm about his tone of voice when he spoke to her.

"Who the devil taught you to get into a boat like that? Don't you have any sense?"

Her cheeks burned with indignation and she struggled away from him. "Look, it's my first boat, all right? I was only trying to do the best I could."

Will stared at her. "You mean you spent summers on the Cape and never once went out on the water? Not once?"

She didn't know why she felt that she had to defend herself. "That's not so unusual. I mean—Uncle Ned didn't like boats. It was enough for me to come to the wharves and watch the fishermen bring in their catch. I didn't need anything else."

Will seemed disgusted. "It figures that old Ned would deprive his own niece like that."

"I wasn't deprived! Ned gave me a lot more than the chance to sail around in some boat."

A determined expression began to settle on Will's rugged features. "Erin, today you're going to find out exactly what you've been missing all your life. After I'm finished with you, you'll never be the same again."

Erin didn't like the sound of this proposition, but she knew that she had to work out something with Will in regard to the *Cape Cod Gazette*. She'd stay on this boat all day, if that was what it would take to make him see reason.

"Look around," he invited, sounding very amiable now. "Make yourself comfortable. A person should always feel right at home on a boat, especially when you're talking about a boat like the *Marianna*." He said the name with a bit of an accent, so that it sounded delightfully foreign.

"Who was the original Marianna?" Erin asked, her curiosity piqued.

"My grandmother. She and Grandpa were both Portuguese, and they came to Jamesport because Grandpa could earn a living here as a fisherman. He built this boat himself—took him years. He never stopped telling us kids that he thought Nana was the most wonderful woman in the world. He said that if you loved a woman you had to name a boat after her, so she'd know that you were serious in your affections." Will chuckled. "They'd been married almost forty years by the time Grandpa finished the *Mar-*

ianna, so I guess Nana just took him on faith until then.''

Erin was intrigued by this glimpse into Will's background, and she looked around the boat with interest. She was surrounded by lovely honey-colored wood, mellowed by time and sea spray. Behind her was the steering wheel, although Erin had a vague idea she was supposed to think of it as the ''helm'' instead. In front of her was the low doorway into the cabin. Duffy the Scottie bustled through it, and it seemed natural to follow him. Erin ducked her head, entering a cozy galley fashioned from more of that beautiful well-seasoned wood. All about her were ingenious cabinets and shelves, along with a fold-down table where the mast thrust into the cabin. Everything was designed to withstand the rocking of gale winds. The table had a raised lip, so plates and cups wouldn't go flying off; an old-fashioned fretted-brass lamp hung firmly from its hook in the ceiling. Erin entertained a disturbing yet compelling vision of herself and Will, sailing out onto the Atlantic for any number of sunlit days...

''What are you thinking about?'' his voice murmured close behind her.

Erin turned around hastily, which proved to be a mistake. There was so little space in the galley that she was virtually pressed up against Will. She drew in a shaky breath and focused her gaze on his chin. It was a decidedly pugnacious chin, and Erin's own argumentative nature was aroused by the sight of it.

''I didn't come to Jamesport to sail off on boats. I came here to run a newspaper the best way I know how—'' She didn't get a chance to finish, for at that moment Will calmly bent his head and kissed her. Just like that...he kissed her. The brim of his cap bumped against her hat, but he didn't seem to mind. Most infuriating of all, Erin herself didn't seem to mind. She allowed her hat to go tumbling off while she arched her neck to take better advantage of Will's kiss.

His lips were gentle yet decisive as they explored the contours of her mouth; his hands came up to cup her face, light as an ocean wave on the sand. Erin found herself trembling in response, and her own hands strayed over the worn cloth of his shirt. She could feel the strong, steady beat of his heart under her palms, and that seemed even more intimate than the way his lips lingered on hers. Some of her common sense returned and she pulled away from him. At least she tried to pull away, sandwiched as she was between Will and the counter. She glared at him.

"Why did you do that?" she demanded.

"I don't know. Why did you?" His tone was solemn, but Erin sensed laughter brimming underneath his words.

"You can't just go around kissing people like that," she informed him, wondering even as she spoke why she felt such a fool. He was laughing openly at her now, in a particularly amused manner. She took a deep breath and tried again. "Look, I don't need this kind of aggravation from you. You're already causing enough problems in my life!"

"Aggravation...so that's what it's called." He fingered a curl of her hair, his hand brushing over her shoulder. His expression became contemplative.

"Your hair looks like it caught on fire from the sun. It's beautiful, Erin."

Will Kendrick was perpetually making her feel off-balance, unsure of which direction she should steer with him. Right now he seemed completely serious, his voice taking on a disconcerting huskiness. But a second ago he had been laughing at her.

The atmosphere in this cabin was becoming much too heated and close. Even Duffy was joining in the spirit of conviviality. After slurping water from a bowl that was cleverly anchored to the floor, he padded over to Erin. He sat down right beside her, his whiskers dripping water onto her foot. Meanwhile, Will was curling another strand of her hair around his finger. Erin decided that the entire Kendrick clan was getting a little too chummy. She grabbed up her hat, crammed it onto her head and marched out of the cabin. But Will and Duffy wouldn't let her escape. The two of them followed her, right on her heels every step of the way.

"You put your hat on backward," Will remarked.

"Oh, drat!" She twisted the hat around on her head, trying to set herself to rights. Now Will was rummaging around in a locker under one of the benches. He tossed her a faded orange life jacket. "Put that on," he ordered.

She took in the briny scent of the life jacket. Like everything else Will owned, it seemed to have endured a long and well-used life. Another few years and the poor thing would probably be encrusted with barnacles but still called on for service. She held it away from her body.

"Look, let's just get down to business—"

"That's what we're doing. We're going to indulge in some businesslike sailing."

She could tell he was still laughing at her. Even Duffy seemed to be grinning, his tongue hanging out the side of his mouth. There was no longer any doubt about it. Erin was being shanghaied by Will Kendrick and his untidy mop of a Scottie!

CHAPTER THREE

WILL BEGAN LOOSENING the mooring lines. "Why can't you just admit that you enjoyed kissing me, Erin? I enjoyed it."

She studied him coolly, still dangling the life jacket at arm's length. "You know, it's interesting that you said those things about my Uncle Ned and women. Whether or not they're true—you're the one who seems to expect a woman to fawn over your kisses and wallow at your feet like some overeager mutt. For your information, I don't wallow." Belatedly Erin realized that her remarks might have sounded a bit harsh to Duffy; her foot was still damp from his fervent dripping. But he was plopped down in a corner, contentedly chewing on a red ball and quite unoffended.

Will, however, didn't seem to share Duffy's philosophical view of life. Looking grim, he confronted Erin. "Don't make the mistake of comparing me to your uncle. I don't need to use women the way he did, and I never make promises I don't intend to keep. As for why I kissed you, I'm starting to wonder about that myself. You're pigheaded and as testy as a groundhog that's missed its nap. I'm trying to figure out what the heck I see in you."

Erin had to admit that she'd never been called "pig" and "hog" in the same sentence before; Will's insults were truly inventive. But at least now he was getting his resentments out into the open, instead of teasing her in that maddening way of his. Erin liked a healthy argument and she jumped right into this one.

"I'm not asking you to see anything in me, Will Kendrick. For all I care, you can think I have the charm of a pincushion. It won't bother me in the least. The only thing I want from you is a little reasonableness where the *Cape Cod Gazette* is concerned."

"As soon as you put on that life jacket, we'll get under way. After that you can spout off all you want about your blasted *Gazette*." His mouth twisted into a wry smile. "Don't worry, nothing personal is going to happen again between you and me. You're an exceptionally attractive lady, Erin, but kissing you isn't worth all the trouble you stir up afterward." With that he dismissed her and went on loosening the mooring lines in order to cast off.

Now was Erin's chance to hop out of this damn boat and find solid ground under her feet again. But she was a fighter, a "scrapper," as her uncle had so often told her. She was going to stay right here and battle things out with Will. She slipped the life jacket over her head, and sat down on the bench with an undignified thump.

A short while later the *Marianna* was sailing the waters of Cape Cod Bay, the old wooden buildings of Jamesport receding into the distance. Will stood with one hand resting easily on the helm. Under his guidance the *Marianna* rode the waves as elegantly as a swan gliding on a pond. The sails had captured the wind in their canvas, billowing out like immense wings. Erin had never realized there could be such beauty in the motion of sails. But it was the intense expression on Will's face that claimed most of her attention. He was definitely enjoying himself, yet she sensed something deeper, too. He looked like a man who had found his true element in life, or perhaps a combination of elements: ocean water, salty air, open blue sky. At this moment Erin couldn't imagine Will Kendrick in any other setting.

He glanced at her. "You might as well go ahead now and say your piece about the wonderful *Cape Cod Gazette*. Let's get it over and done with."

Resentment flared inside Erin. He made it sound as if she'd finally been granted an audience to speak to the king and had three minutes to state her case. But she refused to tolerate his arrogance. She struggled up from the bench where she'd been sitting, lurching with the movement of the boat.

Will grabbed hold of her hand and hauled her over beside him. He looked disapproving. "Don't go jumping around like that. You're ballast, and you should stay put exactly where I tell you. Besides, I don't want to be fishing you out of the ocean." Without ceremony he prodded her down onto the bench that curved in front of the helm. Erin didn't appreciate being referred to as ballast. Will sat beside her, and at least now they were both on a more equal level. She didn't like craning her neck to look up at him.

"I've already started investigating your story about Uncle Ned," she began, keeping her tone brisk and professional. "What I've come up with are several facts. Number one, your Aunt Maggie did apparently lend Ned a large sum of money. Number two, it seems he used that money to pay off several outstanding debts. Number three, he fully intended to reimburse your aunt.''

"Don't be too sure about that last little item. Old Ned would've tried to get away with anything if he had a chance—even robbing a woman of her life savings.''

Erin curled her fingers against her palms. "My uncle was an honorable man! And I'm honorable, too. I want to work out some sort of arrangement with your aunt. But I can't do that if she won't talk to me. I went to her house today, and—''

"You what?" Will's eyes went as hard and cold as onyx. "I told you I didn't want her bothered with all this. She's already gone through enough because of you blasted Lewises. Stay away from her, Erin.''

She didn't answer. He turned the wheel as the breeze stiffened, his attention momentarily diverted. Confound it all, she thought, why couldn't Maggie Kendrick speak for herself? Was the woman going to spend the rest of her life hiding behind the lace curtains of her little saltbox house? Erin was being forced to negotiate with Will as the middle man, and she didn't like it one bit. Then a new thought struck her.

"Will, if your aunt's savings are all gone, how is she paying her bills right now? You're supporting her, aren't you?''

His profile was impassive. "Whatever financial arrangements Maggie and I have made are confidential. All you have to worry about is liquidating the newspaper so you can start to pay her back.''

Will's reticence only confirmed Erin's suspicions. He was most likely handling his aunt's expenses. Now Erin felt a reluctant admiration for Will. She liked the fact that he didn't want to talk about helping his aunt. He refused to brag about his charity; Erin could respect a man like that.

She looked out over the water, hands clasped tightly in her lap. Other boats bobbed along in the bay, some with cheerful sails in yellow, red or green. From a distance the sails looked like brightly colored triangles of paper a child might have used to decorate toy boats.

"Will, I'm not going to liquidate the *Gazette*. That's one thing you'll just have to understand."

He looked stern. "You don't have any other choice, Erin. Lord, don't make me take you to court over this. It won't be pleasant for either one of us."

"All I'm asking for is a little time. A few weeks, that's all, so I'll have a chance to get the paper going again. I promise you, after you see the first issue I put out, you'll know I have what it takes. You'll know I can make the *Gazette* a success, and that I can repay your aunt in the bargain." Erin stopped, breathless. But Will didn't seem moved by her plea. He merely shrugged.

"No sense in you wasting your time with the *Gazette*, Erin. There's no possible way you can turn that rag into a real newspaper."

"I already have my plans laid out. For one thing, I'm going to launch a campaign that will inspire every businessman *and* every businesswoman in Jamesport to advertise in the *Gazette*."

"You're dreaming, Lewis. In the past twenty years or so, Ned managed to alienate practically the whole town. He was always full of grand schemes for the newspaper, and he scammed money from a lot of different people. My aunt was only the last in a long line of so-called investors. No one's going to want to deal with the *Gazette* after that."

"Then I'll just have to convince people to change their minds," she argued. "I'll prove to them that Ned's intentions were good—that his ideals can still live on in the *Gazette!*"

Will gave a wry grimace. "Exactly what do you think Ned's ideals were, Erin?"

"Uncle Ned inspired people, that's the important thing. When he wrote about injustice, he could make you see and feel his own vision for a better world. I've never found anyone else who can do that, anyone who can measure up to him." Erin stared disapprovingly at Will.

"Is that why you're not married? You've been waiting around for a Ned Lewis clone to sweep you off your feet?"

She gazed at a yacht cruising far out on the ocean. "Maybe I do want to find someone like Ned. There's nothing wrong with that. A woman should have standards when she's looking for a male."

"So you're actively looking for a man. That's interesting." The gleam was back in Will's eyes. Erin flushed as if on command.

"I didn't say that. I'm perfectly happy on my own. It's just that when someone potential comes along, I have a way to gauge his qualifications. I compare him to Uncle Ned."

"I hope you spend the rest of your life being single, then. With any luck, there isn't another reprobate out there like Ned Lewis."

"I don't need a man," Erin insisted. "That's the point I'm trying to make, if you'd only listen. I'm a very independent person."

"I've noticed that much, all right," he remarked dryly. "But something tells me you're also a passionate woman, Erin. There's no way you can get around it—that fiery hair of yours is a reflection of what's inside you. It seems to me you do need a man to bring all that passion into the open." Will spoke with utmost seriousness, but a corner of his mouth betrayed him by curving upward just a bit.

"What about you?" Erin challenged. "If you know so much about women, why aren't you married yourself?"

Will lounged back further on the bench. "Well, now. How do you know I'm not married?"

Erin surveyed him thoughtfully. His hair was a shade long, curling at the nape of his neck and behind his ears; apparently he didn't care for the groomer's any more than Duffy did. His shirt was clean but fairly wrinkled in places, and probably had never seen an iron. Everything about him suggested the untamed, the unmanageable.

"You're not married," she affirmed. "Believe me, I can tell. You're not living with anyone, either. No woman could resist the urge to buy you some new clothes or at least hang up the old ones. You probably have a pile of dirty socks that's been sitting in the middle of your living room for three years. Am I right?"

He looked disconcerted for a minute. "Actually the dirty socks are hidden away in a corner of my bedroom. And they've only been there a couple of months." He stretched out one leg and flexed his foot in its disreputable shoe. "As for marriage...I have this philosophy. Namely, if something isn't broken—why fix it? Duffy and I are happy with life just the way it is. We're buried under our own laundry, and we don't want anyone to go poking around in it."

Erin wished she didn't feel quite so happy to know that Will Kendrick was unattached. "I see," she goaded him. "You're the kind of man who'll go to bed with a woman, but you won't sleep overnight at her house because that would be too much of a commitment."

He chuckled. "Don't make too many assumptions about me, Erin. I can promise you one thing. If you ever invite me to stay overnight, I'll be right beside you when you wake up the next morning."

Curse the man, how did he manage this? Twisting her words around to his own advantage! Even in her annoyance, Erin couldn't stop an image from floating through her mind: Will Kendrick's head resting on one of her pillows, his dark curly hair a bold contrast to the whimsical flower design she favored in pillowcases.

Will grinned at her as if he knew exactly what she was thinking. She found herself blushing more furiously than ever. Sometimes she felt as if she had a furnace inside her, periodically being stoked and producing these aggravating flushes. With Will Kendrick, the furnace always seemed to be burning fullblast. She blew out her breath in a futile effort to cool her cheeks.

Will straightened up. "Ready about," he hollered, making her jump. Duffy immediately scrambled to his feet, tail wagging with an air of expectancy.

"What's going on?" Erin asked suspiciously. She didn't like the lazy smile Will was treating her to right now.

"You and Duffy are the crew of the *Marianna,* Erin. It's time you learned something about sailing. Active participation, that's the key to any new skill."

"Oh, no," she protested. "You practically pirated me onto this boat. All I wanted was a business meeting, not induction as a sailor." A familiar unease was rippling through Erin. All her life people had assumed that because of her height and build she was naturally athletic. The coach of the girls' basketball team back in high school had been overjoyed to see Erin . . . until Erin actually tried to dribble a basketball. The truth was, she'd always been gangly and awkward when it came to physical endeavors. She'd already betrayed her clumsiness while boarding the boat. Surely she didn't need to humiliate herself any further. But Will was nudging her inexorably into the position in which he wanted her. He thrust a slender rope into her hand; she was dismayed to realize that the rope was attached to one of the sails.

"Hold onto that," he ordered. "It's the port jib-sheet. But I want you to be ready to tend the starboard jibsheet when I tell you. We're going to be swinging onto a new tack—it has to be done just right so we don't miss stays or, worse yet, get caught in irons."

Erin clenched the rope in apprehension. He might as well have been speaking to her in Portuguese.

"What the blazes are you talking about, Will Kendrick?"

Laughter sparkled in his dark brown eyes. "Just hold onto that jibsheet the way you're doing and everything will be fine. Don't worry, McDuff and I will have you seaworthy before you know it."

Duffy wagged his tail. Will Kendrick and his Scottie were infuriating. She didn't want to be seaworthy. She longed only to get on with the work she'd been born to accomplish—running a newspaper. Erin felt most happy and confident when she was hunched over a computer keyboard, hammering out a story at top speed to meet a deadline. She didn't belong on a sailboat!

"Hard alee," Will called now from the helm of the *Marianna*. "Erin, that means we're going to be shooting straight into the wind for a few seconds. The sails are going to luff for a bit—they'll be shaking. Don't let that worry you. Your one responsibility is to handle the jib. I know you can do it." His voice was calm and authoritative, all the teasing gone. Erin's nervousness began to ebb away and she listened intently to Will's instructions. The boat arced smoothly to the right; under Will's direction Erin released the rope she was holding, allowing the sail called a jib to swing over to the right as well. She took up another rope, the starboard jibsheet, pulling on it until the angle of the sail met Will's approval. The boom of the mainsail also swung over to the right—or, rather, to the starboard side of the boat. The whole procedure was accomplished swiftly and easily. The *Marianna* began slicing exuberantly through the water on a new tack.

"You did a good job, Erin. You're a quick learner," Will complimented her. His words were casual, but as he spoke them an unexpected sense of exhilaration swept through her. Right now she didn't feel clumsy or inept, as she so often did with sports. She felt graceful and very much alive to the wind whipping at her hair, the tang of ocean air filling her lungs. Erin laughed out loud with the sheer pleasure of it all.

"You're hooked on sailing already," Will observed, a note of triumph in his voice. "That's even quicker than I expected."

She struggled to make her expression grave. "This is a mildly enjoyable activity, I'll concede that much. But you can't spend your whole life sailing."

"Why not? What better way is there to spend time?" He pushed back the brim of his cap and gave her an engaging smile. It was a wicked smile, actually, suggesting that he knew at least one other way to pass time besides sailing. Erin's skin heated up. She stared at Will's mouth, remembering his lingering kiss. She swallowed hard.

"Um…a person has to have a purpose in life," she said, her voice coming out with a croak. "I mean, sailing isn't a purpose. It's a pastime, nothing more."

"How can you be sure about that? Maybe it's the only way to discover the true meaning of life. Look at me. I've got my boat yard, Duffy and the *Marianna*. What else do I need?" He leaned back comfortably in his seat, using one hand to guide the boat's wheel. Darn it, he looked so attractive in those faded jeans and old shirt, with his uncombed Scottie perched on the bench beside him. Watching him, Erin forgot what she was doing and the jibsheet jerked in her hand.

"Easy there!" Will said. "You're hauling the jib in too tight."

Erin had to concentrate on more of his instructions, making adjustments so the sail would be trimmed correctly.

"Wait, now you've eased out the jib too far," he warned. "What we're trying to do is create exactly the right kind of space between the jib and the mainsail. A slot for the wind to rush through so we'll have good lifting power and the best speed." He sounded enthusiastic on this obscure subject of wind angles, as if it was the most important thing in the world. Erin herself was getting caught up in all the details of angles, slots and degrees of lifting power. She liked the wild, carefree way sailing made her feel, as well as learning the technical facts like this. She was sharing something exciting with Will Kendrick . . . but perhaps that wasn't wise. Her fingers twitched on the line.

"You keep calling this thing a sheet," she complained. "But it's a rope. A sheet is something you put on a bed. Why not call things by their proper names and be done with it? And you still haven't agreed to my proposal. I want a few weeks without interference from you, so I can get the *Gazette* started up again. What I'm asking is reasonable—and if you're a reasonable man you'll let me get on with my job. You owe me at least that much."

"Lewis, I don't owe you a damn thing." His tone was blunt and uncompromising. Erin tried to think of some new plan of attack, anything that would make Will listen to her. He was obstinate, but surely there had to be a way to get through to him. As if to offer her moral support, Duffy padded over to nestle at her feet. She reached down and distractedly scratched the dog behind his ears. She must have hit the right spot because one of his stubby legs started thumping in response. Erin wished his master was as easily satisfied!

"Why can't you give me a few weeks?" she demanded. "What will it hurt you—what do you have to lose?"

He didn't say anything for a long moment, but his eyes took on the onyx hardness that was already becoming familiar to her. At last he gave her a mirthless smile.

"I'm not going to make any deals with you, Erin. I know what'll happen. When the first couple of weeks are up, you'll ask for a few more—and then a few more weeks after that. Forget it. I've taken a stand and I'm not going to back down. Just accept the fact that you can't win."

Erin glared at Will. Confound him! He sounded so sure of himself, so convinced of her failure. She would prove him wrong, that was all. He wasn't going to stop her from fulfilling Uncle Ned's dreams. Even more important, he wasn't going to stop her from fulfilling her own dream.

"I'm going to make the *Cape Cod Gazette* a resounding success," she told him in a strong, steady voice. "You're not going to stand in my way. Just wait and see, Will Kendrick!"

They stared at each other, the challenge thrown down between them. Duffy gave an uncertain wag of his scraggly tail. But Erin couldn't allow herself to be softened in any way. If Will was going to be this intractable, there was nothing more to discuss.

They headed back toward the shoreline. Erin knew she ought to be glad; soon she would be leaving the intimate surroundings of the boat. But somehow she felt at home on the *Marianna*. Part of her wanted to go sailing on forever, riding the waves in this sturdy hull built by Will's Portuguese grandfather.

She studied Will obliquely. In many ways he seemed such a solid, steady man. He was proud of his rich heritage in Jamesport, and he lived in easy harmony with his past. Yet in other ways he seemed dangerous. His masculinity was powerful and vibrant, his rugged build only emphasized by his worn and faded clothes. She suspected that he could be ruthless, too, if he decided that he truly wished to destroy the *Cape Cod Gazette*.

But Erin wouldn't let him destroy it. No matter what, she would save the newspaper. There was no other choice.

CHAPTER FOUR

ERIN WAS PREPARED TO PARK herself on the stoop for hours, if that was what it took. Somehow she would force Maggie Kendrick to speak with her.

For the tenth time she reached out and rapped the brass knocker against Maggie's front door. It was so early that even the morning glories looked sleepy curled up in their vines; they hadn't yet turned toward the sun. But Erin couldn't afford the luxury of lingering in bed. After her confrontation with Will on board the *Marianna* last week, she'd been working day and night to get the newspaper into shape. With her limited savings, the task was not proving easy. Already she'd spent an atrocious amount to have the old Teletype machine repaired. And the only employee she could afford to hire was a sixteen-year-old high-school boy who pitched in as reporter, gofer, janitor, sports editor, secretary, receptionist and political cartoonist—all haphazardly rolled into one.

Erin stifled a weary yawn and banged the knocker again. She'd been up well past midnight, writing the new "tourist attractions" page of the *Gazette*. She ought to be at her desk right now, finishing the job. But no matter how busy she was, every day she came to knock on Maggie Kendrick's door. This morning Erin was determined not to leave until Maggie spoke to her. The woman would just have to stop hiding from life in her little apple-green house.

Erin lifted her hand to bang the knocker once again, when the door flew open unexpectedly.

"Young woman, I must say that you're persistent. Oh, gracious, you look just like my dear Ned. Remember what he always used to say? You know, how life was a big ripe piece of fruit and we should all dig our teeth into it and suck out the juice. I'm Maggie, by the way. But of course you know that already. Goodness, aren't you going to come in? You've certainly earned your entrance."

Erin found herself swept into the house on the tide of this disjointed yet enthusiastic greeting. Maggie Kendrick wasn't the least what she'd expected. What *had* she expected? She wasn't sure—perhaps a small nervous woman biting her fingernails. But Maggie was almost as tall as Erin herself. She was also slender and quite simply gorgeous. Her fingernails were amazingly long, not showing the signs of even one nibble. They were painted a deep ruby-red and looked like the talons of some exotic bird.

In fact, everything about her appearance reminded Erin of a magnificent peacock. Maggie was draped in a swirling silk robe of turquoise blue; a matching ribbon nestled in the froth of silver-blond hair that was piled high on her head. Her features were narrow, delicate and patrician. If it hadn't been for that pile of hair, her head would have looked too small for her willowy body. But her eyes were big, a lovely hazel in color and ringed by dark lashes that were a startling contrast to her silvery hair. These beautiful eyes seemed to have a life of their own, darting back and forth in Erin's general direction as if reluctant to confine themselves to one particular focus.

"Follow me—we'll talk in the living room," Maggie chattered on. "You know, I've been debating with myself all along whether or not I should speak to you, Erin. You will allow me to call you Erin? Such a lovely name." Maggie hurried ahead of Erin down the hallway. She moved with alarming speed and it appeared that any second she would go careening over onto her face. How could she maintain her balance when she was wearing such spindly high-heeled slippers? But somehow she managed to remain upright, the folds of her robe billowing out behind her like long tail feathers. She led Erin at a rush into a very cluttered room.

"Sit down right over there and I'll be back in a minute with breakfast. You do want coffee, don't you? And some bran muffins. Believe me, Erin, at my age you start giving serious consideration to bran muffins. I am plagued by the specter of cholesterol—truly plagued." With this dire pronouncement Maggie flitted out of the room.

Erin glanced about, but there didn't seem to be any free space for sitting. She started lugging a box away from the seat of an armchair. The contents of the box clanged mysteriously and Erin had to resist the urge to poke around inside. She settled the box on the floor and then sank into the armchair, slipping off her straw hat. Everywhere she looked, she saw unfinished projects. A long strip of plaid material with pins sticking out of it was flung over a sewing machine; a half-completed needlepoint tapestry was draped haphazardly over the back of the sofa. On the table a game of solitaire was in progress, beside a checkerboard where the red checkers were winning. Open books lay scattered facedown on top of the piano. Everything had been left helter-skelter, as if a fire bell had sounded and the room hastily evacuated only moments before.

Maggie appeared again, teetering on her high heels. A tray was balanced precariously in her hands as she catapulted toward the table. Erin tensed, ready to leap up and grab the tray in case it went flying through the air. Her help wasn't needed, however; by some stroke of good fortune the tray landed on the table with scarcely a clatter. The only casualty was one red checker, which skittered off, landing with a "ping" on the dusty wooden floor.

"Erin, I'm so pleased that you kept knocking out there until I was forced to let you in. That's what we must tell Will—you positively forced your way into the house and I had no choice in the matter. Then he won't blame me and we'll all be happy," Maggie finished up in a cheerful tone of voice. But her eyes swiveled warily, as if to search out Will Kendrick lurking in a corner somewhere.

"I'll be glad to take full responsibility for this meeting of ours," Erin assured her, wondering exactly what sort of relationship Maggie had with her nephew. She seemed anxious to remain on Will's good side. A little rebellion against him might be just what she needed!

Maggie popped down into a chair next to Erin's, sitting on a stack of magazines. She crossed her legs, swinging one on top of the other with a wild motion that almost upended the table. One aristocratic foot poked out from underneath her robe. Her toenails were festive, painted the same deep red as her fingernails. She was truly a beautiful woman, her face remarkably fresh and unlined. It was easy to imagine Uncle Ned falling in love with her. But even when she remained perfectly still like this, she kept her eyes darting about as if worried that something interesting might escape her attention. Maggie Kendrick simmered with uncontrolled energy. Erin felt as if she was sitting next to a big colorful firecracker which threatened to go shooting off in any number of directions. The effect was charming and unnerving at the same time.

"This is the very first batch of bran muffins I've ever made," Maggie confided to Erin. "Go ahead, try one. But you must be perfectly honest with me. Are they any good?"

Erin obligingly picked up one of the muffins. It looked rather like a small brown brick. She bit into it, her teeth barely making a dent. Maggie was watching her with a hopeful expression. Erin bore down on the muffin in a valiant effort to gain some headway, but it was no use. It was like biting into a lumpy brown stone.

She pushed the muffin around on her plate, not quite sure what to do next. Perhaps the wisest course would be to try diverting Maggie from the subject of bran muffins altogether.

"Ms. Kendrick, I'm grateful you've consented to talk with me today. There are so many things I want to ask you about Uncle Ned. And we need to discuss the matter of your loan to the *Cape Cod Gazette*."

"First off, I insist that you call me Maggie. I feel as if we already know each other—Ned used to speak about you all the time. It was such a shock to me when he died, you know. The two of us had made so many plans together. I was heartbroken. Now, Erin, I don't mind telling you Ned Lewis was the love of my life. I can say that truthfully, even after three husbands. And three divorces, more's the pity.'' Maggie stabbed her fork at the muffin on her own plate. She managed to nick the surface, nothing more. She would have been better off with a chisel or possibly a jackhammer. After a moment she gave up the attack. ''Oh, well, what can a person do about it all,'' she said with a philosophical sigh. It wasn't clear whether she was referring to muffins or husbands, but she did elaborate on the latter problem.

"Stuart was the only one who paid alimony, mind you,'' she reminisced, her eyes still roving their own unique path. ''I was very faithful about saving up the checks he sent me. And very nice checks they were. Stuart was filthy rich, bless him. But my first husband gambled all his money away. That was Roger. I divorced him when he used our house in North Truro as collateral in a poker game. If he'd won the hand instead of losing it, that would've been a different matter entirely. Where was I? Oh. I was going to tell you about Donald, my second husband. He was poor. Boring and poor. Now, you can have one or the other in a husband, Erin, and you'll do just fine. But the combination is deadly. Your Uncle Ned was different, of course. He was poor and fascinating. No wonder I loved him. He was the perfect man for me. What on earth are you thinking about, my dear? You look positively flummoxed.''

Erin blinked. Maggie had an impressive ability to leap from subject to subject. Following her line of conversation was like traveling at a rollicking speed through a maze. But at least Maggie's view of Ned agreed with her own, contradicting Will's opinion that her uncle had been a worthless womanizer.

Erin settled back in her armchair. "I was just telling myself that you and Will don't look at all alike."

"Goodness, Will takes after his mother. Why she married my pale, listless brother, I'll never know. The two of them seem surprisingly happy for being so mismatched. They run a bookstore together in Boston, snug as clams. Makes you wonder, doesn't it? It's scary what love will do to you sometimes." Maggie dumped two spoonfuls of sugar into her coffee, then looked crestfallen. She peered down into her cup. "Oh, my, I forgot that I'm cutting down on sugar these days. Too late now. Might as well go all the way." With a shrug of her elegant shoulders, she poured a generous amount of cream into her cup.

Erin took a gulp of her own coffee and nearly choked. The brew was potent enough to dissolve the glaze on the china cup. "This is . . . um, strong coffee," she observed when she could speak again.

"Glad you like it. None of that weak, watery stuff for me, thank you very much. If you're going to shock your system with caffeine, might as well do it right. What were we talking about? My dear nephew Will, of course. He's a good catch, that's what he is. Don't you agree?" Maggie's hazel eyes suddenly seemed a bit too shrewd. She focused on Erin long enough to look her over with a speculative expression.

"I hadn't thought of Will in those terms," Erin countered. "Besides, I gather from what he says he doesn't want any woman to catch him."

"Don't listen to him, for goodness' sake. He doesn't know what he's missing. Of course, Will has never lacked for women flocking to his door. That's not the problem, believe me. Did he tell you about Geneva Lacey?"

"No, he didn't." Erin moved in her chair, not sure that she wanted to know the details of Will's love life. Maggie, however, was unstoppable. She leaned forward, her eyes alight as they shifted back and forth in a conspiratorial manner.

"Geneva was determined to marry our Will. I certainly had no objection to the match—Geneva is a fine girl. And she's inventive. She used every ploy you can imagine to get Will to the altar. One day she even went to Ned and had him print up an engagement announcement in the *Gazette*. As far as Geneva was concerned, it was only a slight formality that Will hadn't actually proposed to her yet. Poor Will just about stirred up a hurricane when he saw that announcement, complete with a photo of Geneva flashing an engagement ring he didn't even know he'd given her."

Erin suppressed a smile with difficulty. She wished she could have been there to relish Will's discomfiture. Two of his least favorite things combined— marriage and the *Cape Cod Gazette!* It would've been glorious to see that.

Erin dredged a spoon through her murky coffee. "Maggie, it sounds to me like Will is really a hardened case. I don't know if you're ever going to see any grandnephews or nieces from him."

"Oh, all he has to do is find the right woman. The kind of woman who can actually break down his defenses. Someone like you, Erin. I think you could do the job.''

Erin dropped her spoon in the cup, splashing thick coffee over the rim. ''Will Kendrick and I don't have a thing in common! And we're not exactly the best of friends, either. The atmosphere gets pretty stormy whenever we're around each other.''

''That's a good sign, right there.'' Maggie nodded with satisfaction, her pile of hair bouncing a little. ''When sparks fly between two people, you know that something's definitely going on. I don't know if you realize how happy it would make me, Erin. You and Will . . . it would be like Ned and me having another chance at love. His niece, my nephew. Oh, yes, that sounds just right!''

Erin could hardly believe what she was hearing. The last thing she and Will needed was a matchmaker. But Maggie's eyes had misted over. Most disturbing of all, for the first time they'd stopped rotating. They were immobile, transfixed on a spot somewhere off in space—as if caught by a vision of Erin and Will entwined together at a celestial altar. This was dreadful. Erin set her cup down with a rattle.

''Maggie, Will and I are adversaries. That's all there is to it. And it's because of you, if you want to know the truth—''

''Ned would be so happy. He thought highly of Will. And of course you were always like a daughter to him, Erin. I wish there was some way to let him know what's happened with you and Will. Do you believe in séances, my dear? I've never been to one, but there's always a first time.'' Maggie clasped her hands together, ruby nails gleaming. Any moment

now she'd be calling forth Ned's spirit to announce
Erin's engagement to Will Kendrick. It seemed that
Maggie's matrimonial tactics rivaled even those of
Geneva Lacey. But this whole thing had gone quite far
enough! What Maggie needed was a firm change of
direction; after all, that strategy had worked with the
bran muffins.

"I'm so glad to hear you speak fondly of Uncle
Ned," Erin began, trying to be her most persuasive.
"Somehow I'd gathered you were very upset about the
money you lent him."

"Good gracious no," Maggie exclaimed, success-
fully diverted. "Wherever did you get that idea? Oh—
Will, of course. He's the one who's upset. I knew he
would be, and that's why I didn't tell him about the
money. Ned and I had plans for the newspaper, you
see, and there wasn't any sense in sharing them with
someone else. But then dear Ned suffered that awful
heart attack. I tried to manage on my own as long as I
could, but somehow I ended up discussing my fi-
nances with Will."

Erin was relieved to see Maggie's eyes snap back
into action. However, they swiveled with added energy now, as if Maggie found the subject of money
particularly stressful when it involved her nephew.
What sort of fear had Will Kendrick put into her,
anyway? He was growing more unpopular with Erin
by the moment.

She tried directing the conversation again. "So es-
sentially you made Ned a business loan. The two of
you were planning on revitalizing the paper. But first
Ned had to pay his debts—get his creditors off his
back."

"That's exactly right. The only problem was that Ned owed more money than either of us had bargained for. Interest does tend to accumulate, you know. It took all my savings to clear his debts."

"But that still leaves one major creditor—you, Maggie. We need to talk about the money I owe you. Uncle Ned would've wanted me to repay you, now that I've taken over the *Gazette*."

"No, no, it wasn't meant to be like that. Ned and I were going to be partners in the newspaper. I didn't want anything else. Oh, Erin, I feel so cheated. Ned wasn't supposed to die! His heart was supposed to go on beating forever."

Maggie sounded wistful and forlorn. Erin didn't know how to respond, because she felt the same way. She'd wanted Uncle Ned to live forever, too. She sat with Maggie in silence, the two of them remembering the man they'd both loved.

A racket at the front door intruded on their reflections. The door could be heard swinging open and then banging shut again.

"Hello, Aunt Maggie!" Will's deep voice boomed out. "I finally finished hammering together those trellises you wanted. They're out back."

"Oh dear, oh dear." Maggie sprang up from her chair, almost toppling it over. She hovered uncertainly, her peacock robe fluttering around her. "Can't you hide somewhere, Erin? Yes, I think that would be best. In the closet, that's the safest place. I'll throw a few coats over you, just in case he decides to look in there."

Erin wasn't about to cower in any closet because of Will Kendrick. She stood up and resisted all of Maggie's efforts to push her out of sight. She was facing the living-room door when Will and Duffy appeared there a moment later.

Will stared at Erin without speaking. His mouth drew into a tight, angry line and the muscles of his face went rigid. Gone was any hint of the easygoing sailor she'd glimpsed before; right now he looked as fierce and relentless as a Portuguese pirate. Erin moistened her suddenly dry lips, determined not to let him daunt her.

"Hello, Will," she remarked in a cool voice, her hands steady even though her heartbeat had accelerated at the sight of him. "I see you and Duffy are up and about early this morning."

Duffy wagged his scruffy tail, but Will's expression darkened all the more. "I want you to get the hell out of here right now, Lewis. I'll carry you out myself if I have to. I told you over and over to leave Maggie alone, but you just wouldn't listen."

He took a step toward her. Erin grabbed her hat, as if that would somehow be a defense against him. She wondered if Will would actually attempt to heft her into his arms. The thought tantalized her with its possibilities. Will did look strong enough to succeed at the task, but Erin knew she could give him a good tussle. Darn, she felt herself turning bright pink at the mere possibility of physical contact with him. Erin braced herself as Will took another step into the room. But Maggie seemed to have come up with her own maneuver.

"Will, I want you to try my new muffins!" She grabbed one and started rotating her arm wildly like a crazed pitcher warming up at a baseball game. A second later the muffin whizzed through the air straight toward Will. He looked completely disconcerted, but caught it with a nice backhand grip.

"Go ahead, take a bite and tell me how it tastes," Maggie urged, her eyes darting anxiously. "I'm beginning to think I used a little too much nutmeg."

Will gave Erin another menacing look but for the moment remained standing where he was, raising the muffin to his mouth. Erin watched, mesmerized, as he chomped down on it.

"Aaagh!"

"Does that mean you like it, dear? I'm so delighted. I'll wrap up the whole batch for you to take home with you."

Will's teeth seemed to have embedded themselves in the muffin, and it took him a few seconds to work free of the thing. Then he balanced the muffin on his palm, gazing down at it with perplexity. Erin decided that Will possessed excellent teeth indeed; a lesser man might have chipped an incisor just now.

Meanwhile, Maggie was fussing with the coffee cups, her attention momentarily distracted. Will took full advantage of this opportunity, ducking down and holding out his muffin to Duffy. The Scottie took the muffin in his powerful jaws and scuttled out of the room. Will was just straightening up when Maggie peered over at him.

"Finished already? Good—have another one."

"No, thank you, Aunt Maggie," he answered firmly. "I have business to take care of with Ms. Lewis here." He advanced on Erin again, looking more grim than ever.

"Wait!" Maggie squeaked. She moved to her next line of defense, grabbing the strip of plaid cloth from the sewing machine and whipping it over one of Will's shoulders. With its bristle of pins it made a good weapon, and he winced as it hit him. "Look, I'm almost finished making this muffler for you. But you must hold still so we can have a fitting."

"Aunt Maggie, I think we could safely call this a 'one size fits all.' And you've been sewing this muffler for me for the past five years. It can wait until later." Will lifted away the strip of cloth and handed it back to her. "Stop trying to protect Erin. She's going to have to deal with me sooner or later. She might as well accept that fact, after coming here today like this."

"You can't intimidate me, Will Kendrick," Erin declared, glaring at him. "I'm not afraid of you! And I'm not leaving this house until Maggie asks me to go."

Will scowled. "Forget it. I won't let you harass her another minute. Out, Lewis. Now."

"Seems to me you're the one doing the harassing. You've bullied your aunt until she's afraid to speak her own mind. She wants me to stay. Don't you, Maggie?"

"Oh dear, oh dear. I wish we could all just have a nice little chat..."

"There, you see?" Erin turned back triumphantly to Will. "That's all I want, too—a reasonable discussion. I came here today to work out a satisfactory arrangement with Maggie about the money. Something that will make both of us happy."

Will came close to Erin and grasped her wrist. "I don't want any more talking," he said in a low, ominous voice. "I had my fill of that with Ned Lewis. It's time for action now." His grip tightened on her and he brought his face down next to hers. For an absurd moment she thought he was going to kiss her. Either that, or throw her out of the house. Will himself couldn't seem to make up his mind what he was going to do. He stared at her, his eyes a deep smoky brown. Erin's pulses were throbbing in awareness of him, creating their own sensual beat. Damn it, she wanted him to kiss her, that was the worst of it!

With an effort, Erin wrenched away from him and stepped back. She fanned herself distractedly with her hat. "I think Maggie should decide what's going to happen next," she said, her voice wobbling. She paused, then went on more forcefully. "You keep acting like your aunt doesn't have any say in all this. Well, *I'm* willing to listen to her. This is her house, and it's her money invested in the *Gazette*. If you ask me, she's the one holding all the power, not you."

Will's expression was thunderous. "All I've ever wanted was to protect Maggie's best interest. She'll tell you that. Go ahead, Aunt Maggie. Tell Lewis here what you and I decided together."

Both Will and Erin turned to Maggie, gazing at her expectantly. The pressure of their combined scrutiny seemed almost too much for the woman. Now her eyes were really pivoting, as if a whole beehive of activity was taking place in her head. Erin had the unsettling impression that it would be possible to lean forward just a bit and actually hear buzzing sounds coming from underneath Maggie's pile of silver-blond hair.

"Oh, gracious. I think I'd better just come out and say it. That's what I should do, just say it. All right, here goes." Maggie took a deep breath and clasped her hands together. Her long red fingernails dug into her skin.

"Will, I know we talked about making Erin sell the newspaper so we'd get my money back. Yes, we agreed on that, we really did. But after talking to Erin today, I remembered all the plans Ned and I had for the *Gazette*. I remembered what it was like to go down to the newspaper office and sit at my desk. Ned gave me a desk, you know, and I was going to have a nameplate made up, too. 'Margaret S. Kendrick' in gold letters, that's how I pictured it. You see, Erin, my middle name is Sarah. That's why my nameplate was going to say Margaret S. Kendrick. But maybe it would be better to spell the whole thing out. Margaret Sarah...of course, I never did get my nameplate."

Maggie was going off on a tangent again. But she was so painfully nervous about making this speech of hers that Erin didn't have the heart to interrupt. She waited silently, hoping that sooner or later Maggie would get to the point. Will didn't speak, either, but his posture was tense.

"I used to sit at my desk a lot, down the hall from Ned," Maggie rambled on. "I didn't have a job yet, but I was going to have one. It was all part of the game plan. I never told you this, Will, because Ned died and it seemed like my dreams died with him. But then Erin came along and decided to start up the paper again, and now I think it can happen, after all. I think I can have what I want more than anything in the world." She stopped dramatically.

Erin couldn't tolerate the suspense any longer. "Maggie, exactly what *is* it you want?"

Maggie beamed, showing some decisiveness at last. "My own column in the *Gazette,* of course. You know, so people can write in and ask me for advice about their love lives. What to do about two-timing husbands, boyfriends who flirt with your sister, sisters who sleep with your boyfriend. And men who refuse to get married. Can't forget about that one." She glanced wildly from Erin to Will and then back again. "I want to be right on the second page, where everyone will be sure to see me—'ASK MAGGIE' in all caps across the top, extra-big type. Well, don't just stand there looking addlepated, the two of you. That's what I want—my new career!"

CHAPTER FIVE

MAGGIE'S ANNOUNCEMENT shattered the air like one of her bran muffins crashing through a plate-glass window. At first Erin was too dismayed to speak. Wild-eyed Maggie Kendrick writing an advice column for the lovelorn wasn't exactly her idea of solid journalism. And that was all Erin wanted for the *Gazette*—nothing but good, solid journalism.

Will also seemed to be struck speechless. He rubbed the back of his neck, coughed twice and then fished a piece of rope out of his pocket. Using a great deal of concentration he began fiddling with the rope. His fingers moved with dexterity, creating a knot that was a small work of art. Erin decided it was up to her to get this conversation going again, no matter how disturbing it might be.

"Well, Maggie, this is certainly...uh, an interesting possibility you're proposing. But you haven't had any experience with this kind of thing, have you?"

"Experience! My dear, what about those three husbands of mine? And then I had what everyone called a fling with your Uncle Ned. Goodness, I could write a book about it all. Make that four books."

Erin was eager to try diversionary tactics once again. "Now, there's a good idea! Why not write a book instead? That'll give you a much broader scope.''

"Someday I will write a book. Absolutely.'' Maggie's hair quivered with enthusiasm. "But for now I'll just stick to my newspaper column. I'm so happy that I'm finally going to do this! You know what Ned always used to say. 'Go after your dreams, Honeypot'—that's what he used to call me. Honeypot, or sometimes he'd call me his Jelly Bean. Or Sugar Plum..."

Will groaned. "Aunt Maggie, please—"

"Anyway, that's what he used to say. 'Go after your dreams, shoot for the stars.' Isn't that wonderful advice?''

Erin gave a rueful nod of acquiescence. She'd heard Ned proclaim those words often enough; they'd inspired her to follow a journalism career, her own particular dream in life.

"Aunt Maggie, you've got to be kidding about this,'' Will interjected. "Just because Ned Lewis had some cockeyed scheme about you writing a column, doesn't mean you have to go through with it. Come on, is this what you really want?''

Maggie teetered back and forth on her heels. "Oh, but don't you see? It wasn't Ned's idea in the least. He was all set to have me be his secretary. The dear man was willing to take a chance on me, even though I can't read my own shorthand. I was grateful to him. But then I just started thinking and thinking, and 'Ask Maggie' came to me. There wasn't a thing I could do about it.'' Her eyes rotated in a manner which conveyed the inexorable nature of fate. "It appeared right there in my mind—'Ask Maggie,' second page of the

Gazette, bold type. And it wouldn't go away, no matter what I did. I had to talk to Ned about it and he said it was a marvelous idea. There you have it!''

Will's expression was sour. "Fine. Go write a column for some other newspaper. Any newspaper. But once and for all, rid yourself of the Lewises and that blasted *Cape Cod Gazette*. Start fresh."

"Gracious, I'm afraid that won't do, my dear. Unfortunately one must be realistic about the newspaper business. That was difficult for Ned, you know. He was such an optimist about everything. He wanted to believe that everyone could have dozens of opportunities. I found that quality very endearing in him. Not to mention the fact that he was a superb dancer. Oh, he knew all the dances. The fox-trot, the waltz, the rumba...yes, it was definitely Ned's rumba that captivated me in the first place."

"Aunt Maggie, you were talking about being realistic," Will reminded her in a dry tone of voice.

"Of course." She waved her hands, ruby nails flashing. "You see, William, there isn't much chance another newspaper will take me on as a columnist. My age is against me, for one thing, and Erin is most correct in pointing out that I don't have any writing experience." Maggie shot a glance in Erin's general direction, giving what appeared to be a wink. It was difficult to tell, because Maggie's eyes darted back and forth so rapidly. "No, my one opportunity is with the *Gazette,*" she rattled on. "You see, Erin and I can work out a happy arrangement. For my part, I won't require immediate repayment of my money. That means she won't have to sell the newspaper or do anything distressing like that. For her part, she'll give

'Ask Maggie' a chance to succeed. Ned would've been so happy to hear that, don't you think?''

Erin gazed at the other woman with reluctant admiration. In her own scattered and circuitous way, Maggie Kendrick knew how to work toward a goal. And she was offering a deal Erin couldn't very well turn down.

Will frowned. "Blast it, Aunt Maggie, you can't just throw away all the money you poured into the *Gazette!* That's what'll happen if you do something this crazy."

Maggie's eyes swiveled back to Erin, as if looking straight at Will was proving too much for them. "I'm sure Erin will agree with me that I'm not throwing my money away. As soon as the *Gazette* is on its feet again, she'll start repaying me. Won't you, dear? Meanwhile I'll consider that I've made an investment in my own future. That's what you've wanted for me all along, William. You're such a good nephew. A woman couldn't ask for more. Certainly not."

Maggie was starting to appear frazzled after all this assertiveness of hers; a silvery curl of her hair had escaped its ribbon and bobbed down on her forehead. She bustled over to a shelf crowded with knick-knacks, rummaging about until she found a ring of keys.

"I know what I'm going to do," she exclaimed. "I'm going to leave the two of you here alone to discuss all the details of our friendly arrangement. That would be best, don't you agree? And I'll just hop down to Mr. Beeson's Office Supply and tell him I'm going to need that nameplate, after all. Toodle-oo, now."

Before either Will or Erin could protest, Maggie careened full tilt out of the house, robe billowing behind her. Erin made it to the window in time to see Maggie scrunching her tall frame into the little pink-and-white Metropolitan. She slammed the car door shut on the hem of her robe. The turquoise cloth fluttered in the breeze as the Metropolitan chugged out the driveway; Maggie waved energetically in the direction of the house and then gunned her car down the street.

Erin couldn't help wondering what effect Maggie would have on Mr. Beeson, rushing into his store clad only in her flowing robe and high-heeled slippers. But perhaps Jamesport was already well-accustomed to Maggie Kendrick.

Erin turned from the window to find Will regarding her with disgust.

"Lord, see what you've done now, Lewis. If you hadn't come here today, she never would've got this damn fool idea into her head. You'd better sell the newspaper before anything worse happens."

Erin crammed her hands into the pockets of her corduroy trousers. "Look, you don't have control over this situation anymore. Haven't you realized that? Maggie just declared her independence from you, and I think it's great."

He raised his eyebrows skeptically. "Your emotions are too easy to read, Erin. I could tell you weren't exactly thrilled with the idea of Maggie trashing up your newspaper with a lot of sentimental garbage."

Erin stiffened. All right, so maybe she wasn't ecstatic at the prospect of a lovelorn column. And she had serious doubts about Maggie's ability to confine herself to one subject long enough to give actual advice to anyone who asked for it. But Will had an incendiary way of phrasing things. He made Erin want to defend Maggie at all costs.

"Listen, Will, I think it's about time you started encouraging your aunt instead of putting her down. I know you have some outmoded notion about protecting her from harm. Maybe your intentions are good, who knows. But Maggie needs to experience life, not hide from it. Start treating her like a real person for once. That's what Ned did, anyway. He inspired her to believe in herself."

Will gave a harsh laugh as he walked toward her. "The truth is, Maggie forked over all her money to him and his idea of gratitude was to use her as a secretary. That's really inspiring, isn't it?"

Erin reached out and yanked a dead leaf from one of the geraniums along the windowsill. Unlike the flowers outside, these plants looked shriveled and parched for water, as if Maggie had completely forgotten their existence. Erin pulled off another dead leaf.

"For your information, Will, it's a comfort to have someone refer to my uncle as 'dear Ned' instead of 'old Ned.' Both Maggie and I can't be wrong about him."

Will merely shrugged. "Maggie calls me 'dear William' all the time. Does that make me a saint?"

"I'd say that's the last thing you are," Erin grumbled.

Will stared down at her, his eyes so dark now they looked almost black. She was much too aware of his elemental masculinity. Today he was wearing another threadbare shirt, although it was possible to tell this one had once been a deep shade of blue. Even in its faded state it reminded Erin of the ocean waves that had lapped against the sides of the *Marianna*. She drew her breath in shakily, fighting a longing to be out with Will and Duffy on that boat. It was becoming difficult for her to concentrate on the matter at hand, but she made another attempt at it.

"Will, the point is that Maggie's a lot smarter than you give her credit for. She's making darn sure I don't have any choice but to accept her terms. If I want the *Cape Cod Gazette* to stay afloat, I'll have to let her write this column. That's pretty crafty of her."

His mouth twisted in a wry grimace. "You make it sound like you admire her. But I can see right through you, Erin. All you really care about is your damn *Gazette*. Maggie's just a means to an end."

She flushed with anger. "That's not the way it is at all! Of course I care about the *Gazette*. Running that newspaper is my dream as well as my livelihood. But I don't use people. I respect Maggie's courage. And I feel empathy for her. We both loved Ned in our different ways. We both..." Erin's voice trailed off, and she couldn't remember what she'd been about to say. Will was gazing down at her with a different expression now—a look of unfathomed desire.

"Hell," he muttered, as if giving in to the inevitable. The next thing Erin knew she was swept into his arms, her lips yielding to his. She didn't struggle against him, not even for an instant. She couldn't struggle, because all she wanted at this moment was the soft texture of his shirt under her hands and the salt-spray taste of him against her mouth. The morning sunshine flooded over them as they stood locked

together at Maggie's front window. It was magical
sunshine, a stream of gold enveloping them in their
own private world. When they broke apart, it was only
because neither one of them could survive any longer
without breathing.

Erin drew in air with a gasp. She was still leaning
against Will; as she opened her eyes, dust motes sparkled in the golden light surrounding her. "Confound
you, Will, why do you keep kissing me? It's not fair. I
can't think straight!"

His arms tightened around her. "You do entirely
too much thinking, Lewis." His voice was low and
husky. "Believe me, I don't know why I want to kiss
you all the time. It's something that comes over me
whenever I see you. I figure I might as well enjoy it,
though."

Will's next kiss was slow, unhurried. His lips navi-
gated a sensuous route, moving over her temple and
her cheek. Then he claimed her mouth again, his
hands losing themselves in the wild masses of her hair.
Erin felt as if the sunshine was spreading all through
her body, sparking fire deep inside her. It was a very
long while before Maggie and Will broke apart again.

Erin's legs were as stable as melted butter. She hob-
bled away from Will before he could ravish her any
further. Kissing him could definitely get to be a habit
if she didn't watch herself.

"Maggie is even more sneaky than I thought," Erin
declared. "She didn't just leave us alone so we'd talk
about the *Gazette*. She wanted something else to happen between us. And you know what? We fell right
into her trap!"

"Don't be paranoid. Maggie doesn't have anything to do with this. Why don't you come back here and we'll do a little more experimenting." He smiled, looking roguish and more attractive than ever.

"Oh, no." Erin barricaded herself behind a wing-back chair. "This is more serious than you think. Maggie's decided that you and I should get together. She's talking marriage."

Will's stance changed at this dreaded word. He folded his arms across his chest, frowning in consternation. "Exactly what did the two of you talk about this morning?"

Erin decided not to divulge the knowledge she'd gained about Geneva Lacey. "It seems Maggie sees a pleasing symmetry in you and me. I'm the niece of the man she loved, you're her nephew... somehow that combination appeals to her. She thinks we belong together, as in 'happily ever after.'"

"Good Lord. She's lost the last few marbles she ever had."

He didn't need to sound quite so disgusted. Erin tilted her chin. "Believe me, I don't have any designs on you. You're not my type of man at all. Not in any way."

Now Will looked thoughtful. "That's odd. I could've sworn you were enjoying me a few minutes ago."

Erin gripped the back of the chair, her fingers digging into the upholstery. She was undergoing a frightful temptation to scurry right back over there to Will so she could prove exactly how much she'd enjoyed his kisses. But she couldn't allow herself to succumb.

"I know what I want in a man. And it's a lot more than a mere physical attraction."

Will nodded. "Right, right, you've got to find someone like Ned. But with your idealistic image of him, no one will ever come up to scratch. That's a convenient way to avoid getting close to anyone. Maybe you're just plain scared of men, Erin."

She strode into Maggie's cluttered kitchen, filled a glass of water at the sink, and strode back to the living room. She started dumping water onto the withered geraniums. Perhaps she was a bit too zealous; the poor plants would most likely go into shock after this unexpected deluge.

"I'm no different than anyone else—I have physical needs," she stated. "But I believe in long-term commitment. Old-fashioned marriage, in fact. What's wrong with that?"

Will took out his piece of rope and began tying another knot, his powerful hands adept. "Marriage may be all right for some people, but it sure isn't for me. I'm not going to mess up my life when I'm perfectly content with it."

Erin found it significant that Will had just created a noose with his rope; apparently his misgivings about marriage went quite deep. She shook her head. "It's too bad you won't let a woman get close to you. Someday you and Duffy will start to feel lonely. That's sad—I'm sorry for you."

He didn't seem disturbed by her judgment. Undoing the noose, he proceeded to tie yet another knot. Now his hands moved more slowly. "Erin, I'd let you get close, all right . . . in the way that matters. Sharing something warm, basic and physical. But afterwards the two of us could have our freedom and independence. We wouldn't end up hating each other, and we might even remain friends.''

Erin thought about the earthy relationship he'd just described. And she thought about being in Will's arms for hours instead of only minutes. Mesmerized, she watched his fingers play over the rope. They were strong, blunt fingers that could be surprisingly gentle. She'd discovered as much whenever he touched her. Will Kendrick possessed a seaman's hands and a lover's caress . . .

Erin was trembling. She pressed her arms tightly against her body, trying to quell the heated throb within her. She was really losing control if watching a man tie knots could unravel her like this. But she'd never be happy with a relationship that ended every morning. She could be certain of that much about herself, no matter what provocative effect Will had on her.

"Afraid I'll have to turn down your offer," she said crisply. "I'm looking for something a little more exalted.''

Will smiled. With his dark curly hair and bold eyebrows he looked dangerous right now. "You're lost up there in the clouds somewhere, Erin. Maybe I could teach you a few things about the basic pleasures of life.''

"You're really arrogant, you know that? And you're stubborn, opinionated, mule-brained—''

"I'm back," trilled Maggie's voice from the front door. "I'm sure you have everything all worked out by now. I knew from the very beginning the two of you would hit it off. I just knew it!'' She spun into the room, heels clacking on the floor. Her robe swelled out around her as if she'd been carried in by a gust of wind. Erin was grateful for the interruption. Another minute and she would've bonged Will over the head with one of the flowerpots, just to wipe that self-satisfied grin off his face.

Maggie's eyes swiveled hopefully between Will and Erin. "Go ahead, tell me everything that happened while I was gone. Are the two of you going out to dinner tonight? I know just the place, in Wellfleet. Best lobster you ever tasted. Of course, I ought to call and make reservations for you. Where's that phone book..."

"Maggie, Will and I do *not* intend to share a dinner table tonight. But I believe we've worked out an agreement of sorts. We both realize you have a perfect right to do whatever you want with your own money and time—and that includes writing a column for the *Cape Cod Gazette*." Erin narrowed her eyes at Will, ready to challenge him when he started protesting. But to her surprise, he didn't protest at all. Instead he stretched his arms behind his head and widened his grin.

"That's right, Aunt Maggie, Erin and I have come to an agreement. We know it's impossible to stop you once you've decided to go after something. So we'll just have to make the best of a lousy situation all around. Here's the way it'll work—Erin will start up the newspaper again and you'll write your column. Meanwhile, to protect your investment, I'm going to be supervisor of the *Gazette*."

Erin let out a squawk of outrage. This time he'd gone way too far. "Just a damn minute, Will! No one ever said anything about you supervising me. That's downright ridiculous. I won't stand for it."

"You don't have any choice. And neither do I." He sounded deceptively cordial. "Believe me, I don't want to do this. I'd be happy if the entire *Gazette* building sank into the ocean, never to appear again. But you're right about one thing, Erin—it's Maggie's money, not mine. For some crazy reason she wants the *Gazette* to succeed. The only thing I can do is protect her investment. Ned mismanaged the newspaper, but I won't allow you to do the same thing as long as Maggie's involved. I'm going to monitor every single decision you make."

Erin thumped her fist down on a chair back. "I'm capable of managing the newspaper perfectly well on my own. You can't do this to me! I won't let you do it."

"Wouldn't you say the decision is up to Maggie? You told me yourself—she's the one holding all the power here."

Erin twisted around toward Maggie. Surely in the older woman she'd found an ally, a friend. "You can trust me to run the newspaper well," she stated with conviction. "And eventually I'll be able to pay back all your money. Will doesn't need to concern himself with our arrangement."

"Oh, but it would be wonderful if all three of us could work together." Maggie's eyes gyrated with excitement. "William is such a good nephew to me. If he thinks this is best, he must be right. I've always looked to him for advice. Haven't I, dear?"

He went to stand beside his aunt, hooking an arm around her shoulders. "I'm giving you my advice now, Aunt Maggie. Take me on as the new supervisor of the *Cape Cod Gazette*."

"That has a lovely sound to it, don't you think, Erin? Yes, I believe it does. I want to drink a toast to our new partnership. That's what it is, a partnership between the three of us!"

Erin gazed at the two Kendricks in horror. How could this be happening to her? She'd come to Jamesport eager to carry on Ned's legacy and be her own boss at last. Now she was confronted with a lovelorn columnist gone rampant and a brawny sailor muscling his way into her business. The next thing she knew, she'd have a Scottie ensconced in her office next to the Teletype machine.

Maggie sped back and forth in a whirl between her kitchen and the living room, juggling glasses and a wine bottle. The bottle nearly ended up hurtling through the air, but at the last second Maggie managed to retain her grasp on it. She sloshed wine into three glasses.

"I wish we had champagne, but this will just have to do. I want us to seal our bargain as quickly as possible. Oh, isn't this wonderful?"

Both Maggie and Will took up their glasses. Erin couldn't bring herself to do the same, however. She searched her mind frantically; there had to be another solution, if only she could think of it.

Maggie's beautiful hazel eyes centered on Erin in one of their rare moments of immobility. They had a resolute glint. Maggie seemed especially self-confident when Will was on her side. "We're waiting for you, dear. We can't toast our new enterprise without you."

Will raised his wineglass in a mock salute, looking mighty pleased with himself. "Here's to us, Lewis, and the future."

Confound him. Confound all the Kendricks! Erin gripped her own glass. She hesitated another long moment. But there seemed no alternative. Slowly she brought her glass up to clink against the others. She took only one cursory sip of wine. It tasted bitter to her; even the most expensive champagne would have been galling right now.

Maggie and Will weren't giving her any choice—not if she wanted to save the *Gazette*. She was being forced to capitulate to their demands, but she didn't have to be happy about it. And she didn't have to make it easy for Will.

Erin glared straight at him, lifting her glass a little higher. "Here's to the future," she echoed, her voice grim. "You're getting what you asked for, Will Kendrick. But I can tell you one thing—you're not going to like it! You're not going to like it at all."

CHAPTER SIX

IT WAS GOING TO BE Erin's night. It *had* to be her night, if she wanted the *Gazette* to succeed. She slipped into the ladies' room at the Bayberry Inn. Standing in front of the mirror, she gave herself a quick inspection. She was wearing her best evening gown, a slinky creation in rose-colored silk. It was held up by the flimsiest of straps, hugging the curves of her body but flaring out as the hem dipped toward the floor. The dress followed the sleek lines of gowns worn in the 1930s, and Erin had arranged her hair to be in keeping with this style. She'd gathered back her exuberant curls, subduing them into a chignon at the nape of her neck. Soft finger waves worked into the sides of her hair completed the image of a woman about to go out on the town and enjoy herself in spite of the Great Depression. Erin felt this image was only appropriate. Part of her plan tonight was to project a happy, carefree self while fighting desperately for the *Cape Cod Gazette*.

Over a week had passed since that humiliating morning when Will Kendrick had proclaimed himself her supervisor. The entire time she'd continued working feverishly to salvage the newspaper—meanwhile doing everything she could to avoid Will. She didn't need his interference when there was still so much to do before the first edition of the paper would be ready. The crotchety printing press was acting up again, her sixteen-year-old reporter/secretary/political satirist frowned on using punctuation of any kind, and Erin herself had been overwhelmed with preparations for this evening. She just hoped everything would go according to plan.

Erin sighed in front of the mirror. She needed a few calm moments after her hectic day at the newspaper office; it seemed she could still hear the Teletype machine clattering in her ears. But she couldn't delay any longer. She glided to the door, moving with a grace that wasn't inborn at all. It had taken her years to learn how to carry herself with aplomb. Tonight she was aided by low-heeled silver sandals that were actually comfortable. Shoulders back, head up, she sailed out of the ladies' room—and bumped smack into Will Kendrick.

He was as solid and implacable as a wall of sea rock. His body absorbed the full impact of hers without shifting an inch. He caught her by the shoulders, his hands warm against her bare skin. Erin's first reaction was to lean against him, savoring his nearness. Her second reaction was to pull away and stare at him in indignation.

"What are you doing here, Will?" she demanded. "And you'd better not tell me this is just a pleasant coincidence, you and me running into each other."

"Damn right it's not a coincidence." Will's eyebrows were drawn together in one ominous black line. "You're the one who should be dishing out explanations. I just dropped in on Aunt Maggie and found her holding a séance with the entire Ladies' Auxiliary of

Jamesport. She stopped chanting long enough to tell me how sorry she was to miss the *Gazette*'s grand banquet tonight, but she knew you'd understand. Funny thing is, that was the first I'd heard about the 'grand banquet.' Do you mind telling me what the hell is going on?''

Erin pulled up her dress strap, which had been dislodged by Will's hand. Her skin still tingled from his touch. Was it possible for shoulders to blush? She hoped fervently that it wasn't.

''Look, Will, this get-together tonight is my own business. It's not something you need to worry about. I only invited Maggie at the last minute—''

''I know how you think, Lewis. You didn't want to invite her at all because you knew she'd spill the beans to me. As it is, you're going to be the one spilling the beans. Right now.''

As he spoke, two women edged past him and Erin to reach the door of the ladies' room. Both women frowned at Erin, then gazed at Will as if they'd just pried open a shell and found a delectable oyster nestled inside. Erin suffered a stab of jealousy; she had to restrain herself from pulling open the door and pushing the two ladies straight into the bathroom. What in blazes was happening to her? Now she was getting territorial over Will Kendrick.

Fortunately he was too angry at Erin to notice all the feminine rivalry taking place around him. The two women drifted reluctantly into the rest room after another moment of ogling Will, and Erin ushered him to a more private area down the hall. She opened a door at random, poked her head inside and saw an empty conference room. Good. After prodding Will through the doorway, she confronted him.

"All right, let's make this quick. I don't have much time. What is it you're in such a lather to know?"

"I don't believe this," he muttered. "You know what I want to know."

"No, I don't know what you want to know. And, anyway, I don't think you have a right to know whatever it is *you* think you ought to know."

"Lord." Will ran a hand through his hair. "Come on, Erin, out with it. The whole story. Why is the *Cape Cod Gazette* sponsoring a dinner at a fancy place like the Bayberry Inn?" He shut the door and leaned back against it, closing off the only possible escape route. Erin was annoyed. Did he actually think she was going to try to bolt? She'd been the one to bring him to this secluded spot in the first place.

She hauled up the strap of her evening gown again; it seemed to have developed a tendency to slither downward ever since Will had appeared. "It's very simple. I've invited potential advertisers to this banquet. I didn't see any sense in traipsing to office after office, trying to set up appointments with all these business people. I'll save a lot of time and money rounding up everyone together, and making my sales pitch to them all at once."

"Money—you'll save money? That's what you think?" Will gestured at the surroundings. "Look at this place, Erin. Dollars start falling out of your pockets the minute you step into a joint like this!"

Will was right. The Bayberry Inn was about as high-class a setting as Jamesport had to offer. Erin preferred not to think about the small fortune this banquet was costing her, depleting her savings dangerously, but she'd chosen the Inn on purpose. She glanced about the room. The wainscoting in here was dark old wood that had been cleaned and oiled for a century or more. The wallpaper was equally well preserved, embossed with a pattern of grapevines. And the heavy chairs grouped around the table were plush and inviting in spite of their subdued upholstery; they looked ready to accommodate a meeting of rotund Victorian gentlemen.

"It's a gracious atmosphere, isn't it?" Erin said with approval. "The dining room is even better. Let's face it, Will, all my guests are going to be happy tonight. They'll be full of good food and wine by the time I stand up and tell them about the newspaper. I'll keep my speech nice and short, which should make them even more amenable. Just wait—every single one of them is going to end up paying money to advertise in the *Gazette*. And then all my expenses for this banquet will be repaid twenty times over. You know what they say. You have to spend money in order to earn it."

Will looked at her in disbelief, as if she'd just announced a plan to sail to the moon on the next tide. He started pacing over the dark Persian carpet.

"You're even worse at managing the newspaper than I thought you'd be, Lewis. First off, you started sneaking around behind my back with this chowder-headed dinner of yours. That's the kind of under-handed tactic Maggie uses. Didn't you have the guts to tell me about it to my face?"

There were certain subjects that triggered Erin's temper right off. One of them was the color of her

hair, and another one was any questioning of her
bravery. Even when she was shaking at the knees, she
tried to be courageous. She planted herself in front of
Will so that he had to stop in mid-pace.

"You want to know why I didn't tell you about my
banquet? Because you would've done everything you
could to ruin it, that's why! I don't have the time to
fight you every step of the way. All my efforts need to
go to the *Gazette*. So maybe I'm indulging in guerilla
tactics here. It's much more efficient for everyone
concerned."

Will towered over her, his expression forbidding.
Involuntarily Erin took a step back from him.

"We made an agreement, Lewis. You promised
you'd discuss every single decision with me beforehand."

"I never said that at all," Erin countered. "I listened while *you* said it. You were the one who set up
all the terms and conditions of our so-called agreement."

"That's right. And you're supposed to abide by
those terms, no matter what you think of them. Is that
too difficult for you to understand?" His voice was
belligerent.

"Will, I'm spending part of my own savings to finance this banquet. That makes it a personal decision. It doesn't have anything to do with your status
as my..." She could hardly bring herself to say the
word. But she gritted her teeth and pushed it out of her
mouth: "supervisor."

"You're dead wrong." Will's scowl was truly fear-
some by now. "Anything that affects the *Gazette*—
and therefore Aunt Maggie—is my business. I don't

care if you're spending your sainted grandmother's money. By rights you should be making payments to Maggie, not throwing away your bucks on a harebrained scheme like this.''

Erin blew out her breath in exasperation. "I can't run the *Gazette* without advertisers, it's as simple as that. Unfortunately people won't want to give me money if they think I actually need it. I have to put on a good show tonight. Now, please get out of my way. I have a newspaper to promote.''

She tried to sidestep him, but Will was nimble in spite of his muscular frame. He blocked the path to the door no matter which way she dodged. Then he reached out and captured her waist, his hands anchoring firmly above the swell of her hips. Erin squirmed in his grasp as heat flared inside her. Darn, with his touch so warm on her she was rapidly approaching combustion. But he wouldn't let go. He fingered the silken material of her dress, not an easy accomplishment because the gown was molded so tautly against her body. Erin shivered, captured in a sensuous hot-cold fire as Will pulled the material even tighter across her stomach. If he kissed her now, she wouldn't be able to resist at all. Oh, yes, she ached for him.

But he was looking her over with contempt. "Exactly what is it you're trying to promote tonight, Erin? Something tells me it isn't just the newspaper. You're flaunting your body very effectively.''

Now she burned with a different sort of heat, one of pure fury. Erin wrenched away from him, stumbling backward. She had to resist an urge to cross her arms over her chest. She felt exposed, the silk too flimsy to protect her from Will's ruthless inspection.

"There's nothing wrong with the way I'm dressed, Will Kendrick! This is a fashionable evening gown. What do you think I should do, go out there wrapped in a burlap sack?" She was on the defensive with him, something she hated. Erin much preferred to take the offensive whenever possible. But with Will she was feeling much too vulnerable.

His gaze lingered blatantly on the curve of her breasts. "I'm not complaining about the way you're dressed, Lewis, if that's what you think. This is a pleasurable experience, watching you. I'm sure every other man who sees you tonight will agree with me." His voice had a sharp edge, betraying an emotion Erin couldn't identify. But she wasn't going to be ashamed, no matter what Will Kendrick said. She stood with her arms held loosely at her sides, no longer making any attempt to hide her body from his view.

"For your information, Will, I've worn this dress several times in Chicago and no one thought I was flaunting anything."

He glowered at her, looking like a disgruntled bear. But at least he didn't seem to have anything more to say to her. She smoothed out her dress, pulling up the wayward shoulder strap one more time.

"I'm going to be late, Will. See you later."

He still wouldn't budge. "It's too late to stop this blasted dinner of yours, but at least I can monitor what happens at it. I'm coming with you."

She stared at him in dismay. "You can't possibly do that. Look at the way you're dressed, for one thing."

"What in tarnation's wrong with the way I'm dressed?"

Erin studied his attire. He was wearing jeans that weren't quite as faded as usual, although one knee was patched. Instead of his customary sneakers, scuffed loafers adorned his feet. His shirt appeared to be only a few years old; it was rumpled, but the blue-and-green plaid had yet to be modified by sun or sea spray. Taken altogether, Will had obviously made some effort with his clothes tonight. Erin tried to think of a way to be diplomatic.

"Um, you look great. You really do. But this is a formal event we're talking about."

"No problem." He reached into his pocket and extracted a wadded-up length of cloth. It took Erin a moment to realize what he'd produced was a tie. The thing looked as if it had been used to play tug-of-war with his dog.

Will stalked over to a gilt-framed mirror hanging against one wall. Glaring at his own reflection, he slapped the tie around his neck and proceeded to wrestle with it.

Erin began to be afraid Will would strangle himself. She went over to him. "I'd better help you with that—no, stand still for a minute, would you? Goodness, I thought you were an expert with knots."

"Something about a tie always does me in. Can't tolerate the things." He sounded grouchy, but allowed Erin to take charge. Erin worked slowly and carefully with the tie, determined to finish up the job just right. She made a small adjustment here, gave a short tug there. When she was satisfied, she reached her hands up behind Will's neck to smooth down his collar. Only then did she realize what an intimate act this could be, knotting a man's tie. Even after she'd straightened Will's collar, she couldn't seem to move her hands away from his shoulders. They were so broad and strong, their muscles tensing under her fingers. Erin stared at Will's throat, suddenly afraid to look into his face. But she knew he was gazing down at her. At last she lifted her head.

His dark eyes were mysterious in the shadowy lamplight of the room. Will Kendrick was a man who enjoyed the simple things in life—sailing on a sunny afternoon, relaxing with his Scottie. Erin had learned that much about him. But now she sensed there were depths and complexities in him she hadn't even begun to understand. She felt uneasy and exhilarated at the same time, standing this close to him. Part of her wanted to run away from him, part of her wanted to stay forever.

"Erin..." As he said her name, there was an urgency to his voice, perhaps even a yearning.

She moistened her lips with the tip of her tongue. "Yes?" she murmured, her fingers curling on the plaid material of his shirt.

Will continued to gaze down at her with an intensity that shook her. He seemed on the verge of saying more, but then he gave an impatient shrug.

"It's nothing," he said, his tone gruff now. Erin felt as if he had shuttered himself away from her, in case she tried to get too close to him. But even so, something had flashed between them for a moment—something that went far beyond physical attraction. Surely Will had sensed it, too! Why was he withdrawing emotionally from her?

Erin dropped her hands quickly from his shoulders. Her breath was coming unevenly and she struggled to steady herself. She felt a strange emptiness now that the contact between them had been broken.

Will yanked his tie. "You did a good job with this," he remarked, in an offhand manner that sounded forced. "Seems like you've had a lot of experience."

Erin cleared her throat and attempted to sound equally casual. "Not really. I have a fedora, and every time I wear it I get the urge to wear a tie. And sometimes suspenders, depending on what kind of mood I'm in."

"Hmm...is that a fact? I think you'd look good in suspenders."

"Thank you."

"Anytime."

Erin decided she'd rather fight with Will than endure this restrained politeness. "We might as well go in to dinner," she snapped. "Seeing as you've decided to barge into the middle of things."

His jaw took on a pugnacious set. "Damn right. You're not getting away with anything behind my back."

"Well, then." Erin marched to the door and flung it open. In spite of the tight gown hindering her legs, she was halfway down the hall before Will caught up to her.

"Take it easy, Lewis. We might as well make this a joint entrance. After all, we're both representing the *Gazette*."

"Hmmph." Erin glanced over at him suspiciously as he held his arm out at an awkward angle. He looked like a football player about to charge his way through

a tackle, but Erin deduced that he was offering his arm
to escort her. After a second's hesitation she tucked
her hand into the crook of his elbow, and the two of
them stepped into the dining room of the Bayberry
Inn.

More Victorian splendor greeted them. All the
woodwork was stenciled in gold, the draperies were of
heavy crimson velvet and huge Chinese vases were
scattered about. Already most of the tables were filling up with people.

"What did you do, invite every single warm body in
Jamesport?" Will paused with Erin just inside the
wide double doors.

"I invited anybody and everybody who owns a
business. Or provides a service. Or just plain has some
money to spend on a worthy cause." Erin glanced
around the crowded room, prickles of nervousness
traveling her spine. The field of public relations was
not her favorite one, by any means; neither was
bookkeeping or dealing with suppliers, for that matter. She much preferred to be out chasing down news
stories. But as owner of the *Gazette* she would have to
do it all. There wasn't any other choice.

She gripped Will's arm a little tighter and looked
over at him. In spite of the care she'd taken with his
tie, it was so wrinkled that it hung permanently askew.
His hair was as uncombed as his dog's, and the
expression on his face could only be termed sour.
Somehow all of this contributed to making him the
most handsome man in the room. To be with him gave
Erin an unexpected surge of pride. She propelled him
toward a table at the head of the room where only a
few people were seated. Will looked as if he was about

to complain about something, but Erin didn't give him a chance. She prodded him down into a chair at her left, while she remained standing to welcome her guests.

They all stared at her, their faces seeming oddly disembodied in the dim light. Erin realized she'd stirred up a lot of curiosity in Jamesport with her dinner invitations; she hadn't revealed to any of the guests what her purpose was in bringing them here. Therefore it was natural for everyone to be examining her with interest and expectancy. But she'd hoped to be a little more self-composed when confronting all these people. The encounter with Will had suffused her skin with a rosy glow to rival the color of her gown. She felt like a big pink lamp with enough wattage to light up the entire room.

Erin picked up her soup spoon, trying to concentrate on what she wanted to say. Next to her, Will drummed his fingers on the heavy linen tablecloth, then lifted up a corner and bent down to peer under the table. What on earth was the man up to? His actions galvanized Erin into speech.

"Ladies and gentlemen, I'm so pleased you could attend the first annual *Cape Cod Gazette* business leaders' banquet gala. I want you to have a wonderful time tonight while you celebrate with me the *Gazette*'s brand-new future in Jamesport. So, please—eat and enjoy. This night belongs to all of you." Belatedly Erin realized she was waving her soup spoon around, and she dropped it onto the table with a loud "clack."

After a pause there was a perfunctory smattering of applause; it was obvious that Erin hadn't bowled anyone over yet. She'd just have to count on the food and wine to produce the necessary joviality before she made her sales pitch. She sat down, ready to pull her chair up to the table. But Will had risen to stand behind her and slid her chair in smoothly. She was surprised and impressed to know that he possessed such gracious manners.

"Thank you," she murmured, then turned so she could speak to the man on her right. But Will didn't sit down again. He leaned over her chair and started muttering grievances in her ear.

"What's this claptrap about the *Gazette*'s first annual gala? These people are going to expect you to feed them every year from now on! And why the hell do you have me sitting next to Cynthia Jarrett? The woman's lethal."

"Just sit down!" Erin hissed. Will's hair was tickling her ear, and the warm sensation of his breath on her cheek was destroying all her concentration. He gave a beleaguered sigh that was especially distracting. But at last he returned to his own chair.

Erin did her best to give a welcoming smile to the others seated around her. She'd reserved this table for some of the most prominent business people in town. Across from her was Calvin Draper, a slight man with pale, wispy hair that stuck out on his head like the down of a baby chick. Already he'd unfolded his napkin and tucked it into his collar. There wasn't anything imposing about Calvin's appearance; he wore a powder-blue polyester leisure suit with contrast stitching on the lapels. It was hard to believe that he was a very wealthy real-estate broker.

Next to Will sat Cynthia Jarrett, who owned an exclusive jewelry store in town. She looked as if she might have been gold-plated herself, her voluptuous body encased in an amber sheath deceptive in its simplicity. That dress had probably cost enough to finance a decade of *Cape Cod Gazette* annual galas. Even Cynthia's skin had an amber cast, like the color of rich gold. At the moment she was snuggled up next to Will, talking to him in a low voice. She didn't seem to mind when he didn't answer her. Taking a cracker from the breadbasket, she bit into it with delicate sensuality. "Mmm," she murmured with half-closed eyes, as if savoring an aphrodisiac. If she was this inventive with an ordinary cracker, what would happen when the main course arrived? Erin could only wonder. Meanwhile, Will was just sitting there with a pained expression on his face. Erin was relieved at his lack of enthusiasm, then asked herself grumpily why she cared so much about his reaction to Cynthia Jarrett.

"I must admit you have me very intrigued, Ms. Lewis," remarked a well-modulated voice to Erin's right. "I don't know when I've been quite so fascinated by a woman before."

Good heavens, she'd almost forgotten about Roger Paxton, her most influential guest of all! He owned several art galleries and antique stores on the Cape. He was also heir to the Paxton family fortune. Erin swiveled toward him with her most encouraging smile already in place.

Roger was in his late forties, with a mashed-up face like a boxer who'd seen one fight too many. His unabashed ugliness had its own particular charm, and

Erin found herself instinctively relaxing. She didn't mind flirting a little.

"What is it you find so intriguing, Mr. Paxton? I'd be happy to satisfy your curiosity on any point."

"Give me a break," Will interjected loudly from her left. He nudged her with his elbow for added emphasis. Erin managed to kick his shin under the table and at the same time go on smiling at Roger Paxton. This required a rather severe contortion of her body—but she managed it.

Roger leaned closer to her. He smelled of subtle, expensive cologne. His clothes were also subtle and expensive—dark suit, fine white shirt, silk tie. "Ms. Lewis, you're playing a game with all of us here tonight. You want our money, but you won't come right out and ask for it. That's a very smart business technique. You're beautiful and, I suspect, capable of driving a hard bargain. That's a combination that intrigues me. I'd like to know you better."

Erin didn't feel attracted to Roger Paxton, but she liked his courtly manner. The way he acted, the way he dressed, his career as an art and antiques dealer—all these seemed at odds with his prizefighter's face. Yet the contrast was somehow a fitting one; it didn't jar the senses.

"Mr. Paxton, I truly hope we can become friends."

"Hello there, Paxton," Will interrupted, reaching across Erin to shake hands with the other man. "Thought you'd be interested to know that I'm on board the *Gazette* now."

"Interesting," Roger commented, with a thoughtful glance at Erin. "Don't tell me you're an apprentice in the newsroom, Kendrick. I thought no one could convince you to get off your boat. Ms. Lewis must have a great deal of influence with you.''

''Let just say I've taken on a management position. Erin's my employee, not the other way around.''

Erin gripped the butter dish, wishing she could dump it right on Will's head. What was the matter with him? Even another good kick in the shin didn't faze him. He just grinned across at Roger Paxton, behaving as if he owned Erin. At this rate he was going to ruin all her chances to win advertisers for the *Gazette*. She needed to operate as a woman of power, or no one was going to have any faith in her.

She twisted around in her chair to berate Will in as much privacy as possible, and saw the smoldering look in his eyes. Then the truth struck her, and she recognized the emotion underneath his false geniality. She forgot the insults she was going to growl at him. For all his talk about freedom and independence, Will was suffering an old-fashioned bout of jealousy.

That was it, simple and clear. Will Kendrick was jealous.

CHAPTER SEVEN

CYNTHIA JARRETT SPEARED a morsel of marinated flounder and brought it up to her mouth. She sighed and chewed at the same time, gazing soulfully at Will. He ignored her, sampling his own fish with a critical frown.

"Not bad. But not great, either. This isn't authentic *escabeche,* the way my grandmother used to make it."

"I remember her cooking," said Roger. "Erin, Mrs. Marianna DaSilva was famous in Jamesport. She owned a little restaurant over on Market Street, and people came from all over the Cape to sample her food."

"That's wonderful. Now, Mr. Paxton—I mean, Roger. Let me tell you about my plans to redesign the *Gazette*—"

"You know, I think the recipe for this rice was stolen directly from my grandmother," Will commented. "But it doesn't have enough eggplant. What's your opinion, Erin? How do you feel about eggplant?"

"I hate the stuff." She glared at him. For the last half hour he'd disrupted every one of her efforts to talk about the *Gazette*—or about anything else, for that matter. Her only accomplishment had been to reach a first-name basis with Roger Paxton, and even that had been difficult with Will constantly interrupting the conversation. Now it turned out he was an expert on every dish served by the waiters. Erin was beginning to regret that she'd requested the Bayberry Inn to serve its Portuguese menu tonight. Darn it all, she'd probably been thinking about Will's dark eyes and tousled black hair; otherwise she would've ordered something bland and safe for dinner.

Nothing was going right. Roger Paxton seemed quietly amused as he glanced from Will to Erin, as if he sensed all the undercurrents between them. Cynthia Jarrett continued to sigh and nibble suggestively on her flounder, for Will's benefit alone. Across the table Calvin Draper resisted all attempts at conversation and devoured his food with methodical intensity. He'd cornered the breadbasket for himself and guarded it with care. Erin found it unsettling that such a small man could eat so much, so quickly.

And now, before she was ready, dessert was being served and it was time for her to give her speech. She wanted to address her guests while they were savoring their banana soufflé.

Erin struggled to her feet, waiting for the chatter and laughter in the room to die down. "Ladies and gentlemen," she began, trying to remember the words she'd carefully rehearsed. But all she could think about was Will Kendrick and the way he was turning her life upside down. What had she done to deserve him?

Everyone was staring at her, Will included. She took a deep breath and started again. "You've heard it said there's no such thing as a free lunch. Turns out there's no such thing as a free dinner, either. Now you have to listen to me talk in payment for your food."

Dead silence. Erin gave a quick laugh so her audience would realize she'd made a joke. More dead silence, unrelieved by even a snicker or twitter. Granted, Will's mouth did quirk upward a bit at one corner.

"Yes, well, I want to tell all of you about the new *Cape Cod Gazette*," Erin plunged ahead. "The *Gazette* will resume as a weekly newspaper, but everything else about it is going to change. The next time you pick up a copy of the paper at the newsstands, you won't recognize it. You'll see attractive, easy-to-read pages instead of cramped columns of type. You'll see the top national stories, as well as important local news and a special sight-seeing guide to attract tourists. You'll see commentaries and reports on all the issues that concern you—the environment, the economy, your children's education, rights for the elderly and handicapped. And you know what else you'll see? Other people reading the *Gazette,* many other people, including all the visitors who come to Jamesport. Surely you'll want to advertise in the newspaper so all those readers will know exactly who you are."

Erin paused, looking at the impassive faces before her. Somehow she had to stir a reaction. She took another deep breath. "Ladies and gentlemen, Mr. Will Kendrick's Boat Yard is already eager to advertise in the *Gazette.* He knows this newspaper is going places. Let's all give him a big hand!"

Will stared at her with an expression of complete outrage. She smiled back sweetly and started clapping her hands. Unfortunately not a single person in the audience contributed to her applause. She clapped by herself for a moment, then cleared her throat forcefully. "I hope all of you will join Mr. Kendrick as advertisers in the *Gazette*. It will be a wise decision you won't regret. For now, please enjoy the rest of your meal. And take a turn on the dance floor over here, to the music of Jerry Vane and His Orchestra. I'll be available for anyone who'd like to chat with me." Good grief, she sounded like a cocktail-lounge hostess instead of a serious journalist. But she was finally getting a response of some sort. Several couples moved with alacrity to the dance floor.

Will stood up and leaned close to her, his expression thunderous. "Dammit, Lewis, are you going bonkers? I never said anything about advertising in the *Gazette!*"

"Too late now," she murmured. "Everyone knows you're going to do it. I think a full-page ad would be really nice, don't you?" Before he could protest any further, she turned to Roger Paxton.

"Roger, let's dance," she said, giving him no chance to refuse. She dragged him out on the floor among the other couples. At last she could have a private conversation with him. And she might as well be direct. Trying to soft-sell her newspaper to the Jamesport crowd wasn't proving effective enough.

"How about it, Roger? Let's set up an appointment to talk about an advertising program for you. I have some ideas for layouts that are very eye-catching. Although of course I'd be glad to work with your own people on any ad designs you already have in mind."

Roger maneuvered her at a sedate pace around the dance floor. "You believe in working fast, don't you, Erin?"

"That's because things are going to move fast with the *Gazette.* I wouldn't want you to miss out on any of the opportunities."

His battered features creased into a smile. "Usually I make my own opportunities. And I never like to be in a hurry. People make bad decisions when they're in a panic."

Erin fumed inside while struggling to maintain a calm, pleasant exterior. Perhaps Roger Paxton could take his leisure making decisions. He had a good-sized safety net, with that family fortune of his. But Erin couldn't afford the luxury of time. She had to get the *Cape Cod Gazette* rolling again. And that meant she had to have some advertisers!

Will jogged past with Cynthia Jarrett draped around him in all her gold loveliness. He gave Erin a mock salute which severely tried her patience. She wanted to yell out her exasperation. Couldn't anything tonight go the way she'd planned?

Even Jerry Vane and his ten-piece orchestra weren't what Erin had bargained for. They'd come highly recommended by the inn caterer, and Erin had been so busy that she'd taken the recommendation on faith. It turned out Jerry Vane was a lanky accordion player who seemed constantly on the verge of losing a battle with his instrument. Even though his feet were planted firmly on the floor, his body wove about at odd angles as he grappled with the accordion; he looked like someone pulling a difficult batch of taffy. Somehow Erin had expected something more dignified from

Jerry Vane—perhaps a violin. Even a trumpet would have done nicely. Oh, well.

Behind Jerry was what appeared to be the ten-piece orchestra. A harassed-looking man had a kazoo dangling from his mouth, cymbals strapped to his knees and maracas bobbing up and down in one hand. With the other hand he periodically thumped a long pole against the floor. The pole had three kinds of bells and two sets of snare drums attached to it in a most ingenious manner. On one side of the man was a xylophone, on the other a large gong. Erin didn't even want to speculate how he was going to get a handle on these two additional instruments. But now and then he did manage to exchange his maracas for drumsticks, and that was when the music really became lively.

"I take it you and Kendrick are personally involved with each other," Roger said as he led Erin in a competent but restrained two-step to the rhythm of the maracas. "I suppose that means you won't consent to have dinner with me on Saturday night."

"Look, you don't really think Will and I—that's ridiculous. We're not involved in the least. Maybe we're connected in a roundabout professional way, but that's all." Erin was flustered, couldn't understand why she was flustered, and felt more out of sorts than ever. "Certainly we can meet Saturday night, if you'd like to discuss business then."

"I was thinking more in terms of a date than a business meeting, Erin. There *is* something between you and Kendrick, isn't there?" he insisted. "I always prefer to know what I'm up against."

Erin was turning red with frustration. "Roger, there's nothing between Will and me. Absolutely nothing."

Just then Will tapped Roger on the shoulder and grinned at Erin. "Mind if I cut in? We'll just trade partners here." Deftly, before anyone could protest, he transferred Cynthia into Roger's arms and whisked Erin away.

"Confound you, Will Kendrick, are you going to interfere with everything I do? I almost had a dinner date set up with Roger!"

"Why the heck do you need to go to dinner with him? Just rent a megaphone and announce to the world at large that he's going to advertise in the *Gazette*."

Erin craned her head back so she could frown up at Will, but this proved to be a mistake. It was dangerous to put her body at an incline, for he whirled her around until she thought she was going to flip over backward. Other dancers made room for them as they zigzagged around the floor. Even the snare drums of the one-man band seemed to be rattling at a faster beat now, inspired perhaps by Will's energy. Erin hung on to him for dear life, her head beginning to spin as well as her feet.

"Will, slow down!"

"I can't. Once I get going like this I'm never quite sure how to stop. Aunt Maggie's the one who taught me how to dance, you know." He seemed perfectly serious, but his face was something of a blur so Erin couldn't analyze his expression as carefully as she would have liked. Everything flashed by—Calvin Draper still seated at the table, apparently working on his second or third helping of banana soufflé; Cynthia Jarrett twined around Roger but twisting her head to gaze tragically at Will.

Then Erin couldn't concentrate on anything but keeping up with Will. He seemed to be having a wonderful time as he hummed along with the music. Not only was he off-key, but he was an atrocious dancer as well, constantly in danger of trampling Erin's feet as he whirled her around. So why was she having such a good time? She was grinning idiotically, convinced that any minute she and Will would go swirling off together into space, carried by their own momentum. And she wanted to swirl off with him, lost forever in his embrace.

Jerry Vane and his ten-piece orchestra ended their lively jig and began a more relaxed number. Perhaps this was for the best, because both musicians looked near the point of exhaustion. Jerry appeared to be the worse off of the two, even though he only had to contend with the accordion.

Will proved himself quite capable of dancing at a slow, romantic shuffle. He drew Erin close in his arms, resting his cheek against her hair. Oh, darn. It was delicious to be with him like this. It was heavenly. She succumbed completely to the pleasure of holding him, of being held.

"You can't start going out with Roger Paxton," he murmured in a husky voice. "You know that, don't you?"

Erin breathed deeply, taking in Will's clean scent. He smelled like sea spray and warm sand dunes, like canvas sails whipping out into the wind. No fancy expensive colognes for him . . . she was glad of that. But she stirred in his arms.

"Will, I can handle Roger on my own. If you'd just let me do my job tonight, I'd be able to convince him that he wants a business relationship with me—not a personal one. But whether or not I choose to date anyone is hardly your concern, so why am I even telling you this?"

"Because you know it *is* my concern." His hand moved in a gentle yet sensuous circle over her back. "I want you, Erin," he said in a low voice, the words simple and matter-of-fact. "Lord, I suppose I've wanted you since the first time I saw you sitting behind that blasted desk, the sun coming in through the window and turning your hair into fire."

His touch seemed to melt right through the thin material of her dress, reaching her too deeply. It would be so easy to acknowledge her own desire for him. It would also be very dangerous. Erin stiffened, pulling away.

"A casual relationship, is that all you'd like with me, Will? We'd sleep together and then go our separate ways. No ties, no promises." She kept her tone mocking. "Of course, I'm not allowed to date Roger Paxton or any other man. The freedom will all be on your side, I suppose."

Will moved Erin away from the dance floor and into a shadowy corner of the room. He gripped her arm. "Dammit, Erin, I'm a reasonable person. I believe in one relationship at a time. That would go for me as well as for you."

Erin leaned back against the wall, trying to put some distance between them. "I understand what you're really saying. For you it's like driving one car at a time. But when the car breaks down you have to buy another one. Planned obsolescence, isn't that what it's called?''

At first only his angry silence answered her. The accordion music sounded plaintive and haunting now, like an echo from another era. Will was still holding on to her and she could sense his tension.

''What do you want me to tell you?'' he demanded finally. ''Do you expect me to promise undying love and devotion? Sure, I could say that and anything else you want to hear. But I believe in being honest, Erin. I don't know how much I can give. I can only tell you that you're the most desirable woman I've ever known.''

Erin was caught between yearning and indignation. ''You're making too many assumptions about what I want from you,'' she declared. ''You're just not my type. You don't believe in any ideals that I can see, you're domineering, you're thick-brained and incredibly stubborn. After all that, tell me exactly why I'd want your undying love!''

He made a sound that was somewhere between a snort and a snarl. ''You're the one who's stubborn, Lewis. You think everyone has to measure up to some impossible version of that old goat, your uncle. You refuse to see life the way it really is. But you're going to miss out on a lot if you keep your head in a bunch of clouds that don't have any substance. You're right, I sure as hell don't fit into your idealistic little world. But maybe I'm exactly what you need for a change.''

And with that he kissed her, pressing her against the wall. The planes of his body were hard and powerful, forcing her own softness to yield to him. His lips took hers with exquisite mastery. He was ruthless in the sensual and calculated way he aroused her passion, his hands moving down in a slow caress to her hips.

The shadows enveloped Will and Erin, the music playing unheeded around them. With a small moan she arched her head back, lacing her fingers behind Will's neck to guide his movements. He kissed the pulse throbbing at the base of her throat, just as she longed for him to do. But then he returned to her mouth, no tenderness to soften his demands. Erin clung to him. She returned his kiss eagerly, wantonly, asking no gentleness from him.

Erin was out of control, but she couldn't stop. She was spinning into a world where only she and Will existed, where only the two of them mattered. She couldn't turn back....

But Will wasn't out of control, damn it. He chuckled softly against her mouth. "Yes, Erin, I think this is exactly what you need. And lots of it."

She felt as if she'd been hurled abruptly back to earth. How could she have let herself get so carried away with this aggravating, infuriating, impossible man? And how could she have let it happen right here in the middle of the Bayberry Inn, where she was supposed to be courting advertisers! This was too humiliating.

With an incoherent oath she pushed past him and marched unsteadily toward the dance floor. Her lips felt lush and full, unsatisfied. She made herself walk a little faster, refusing to look back at Will.

Roger Paxton intercepted her smoothly. "May I have another dance, Erin?"

"Yes, of course." She tried to switch into her pleasant, businesslike mode but wasn't overly successful at it. Drained from her encounter with Will, she wanted only to go home and forget the miserable fiasco of this evening.

Roger's expression was shrewd, as if he knew too much about Erin and Will. Maybe he'd seen too much. "I believe we'll have to delay that dinner of ours," he said. "I like the odds to be in my favor when I pursue a woman."

Erin managed a debonair smile. "Surely we can be friends, Roger. And I know you could benefit tremendously from advertising in the *Gazette*. How can I convince you of that?"

He shrugged. "Prove to me that you really can sell newspapers. Prove to me that the *Gazette* is actually going to change, and people are going to start reading it. After that—who knows? We'll talk about it."

This was her one accomplishment so far tonight. One solitary Cape Cod businessman was tendering a vague promise of talk. She didn't even know if she could con *Will* into advertising in the *Gazette*. Meanwhile the accordion played on. The weary but valiant one-man band gave the gong a mighty "thwack" and then scrambled for his maracas again. The business people of Jamesport danced to the music as if they didn't have a care in the entire world. And Calvin Draper sat at the table and turned the breadbasket upside down, his lips pursed in disappointment when nothing fell out.

Somehow Erin had to shake up this town with her newspaper. And she had to shake up Will Kendrick in the process. He was the true source of all her problems. Right now he was watching her sardonically from the edge of the dance floor, Cynthia Jarrett stuck to him like a beautiful golden leech.

Erin stared right back at him. And even though she was talking to Roger Paxton, her words were really meant for Will. It didn't matter that he couldn't hear them.

"Very well, Roger. You and I have a deal. I'll prove to you and to every last person in Jamesport that the *Gazette* is going to succeed. Even more important... *I'm* going to succeed."

A FEW AFTERNOONS LATER Erin pushed her bicycle along Main Street, past shops and restaurants housed in old clapboard buildings. Usually she would stop to enjoy all the details—the striped awnings shading the store fronts, the architecture embellished with tower rooms as well as dormer and bay windows. Today, however, Erin was intent on finishing a job. The wire basket fastened to her handlebars was still half full of flyers. She stopped to tack one of them to a wooden post.

"What do you know, Duffy," Will's voice drawled behind her. "It's our good friend Erin Lewis. But it's not enough for her to throw wild parties at the Bayberry Inn. Now she's desecrating public property, too. This is some active woman. Don't you agree, boy?"

Erin jammed her box of thumbtacks back into the pocket of her khaki shorts. Then she swiveled around to confront Will. Today he wore a T-shirt that was exceptionally faded but which emphasized the muscles of his broad seaman's chest. He also wore a lazy smile that she found exceptionally provoking. She studied him, her eyes narrowed with suspicion.

"Have you been following me, Will Kendrick?" she demanded. In response, he continued that maddening conversation with his dog.

"McDuff, you and I were out for an innocent stroll when we spotted Lewis here across the street from us. Right away we knew she was up to no good, so of course we had to investigate. Isn't that exactly the way it was, boy?"

Duffy wagged his tail and gazed up at Erin, his bright eyes peering out from all that tangle of hair. Why did this rag mop of a Scottie have to be so appealing? It wasn't fair that his owner was so darn appealing, as well. With reluctance Erin propped her bike against one of the storefronts and bent down to pet Duffy. She was rewarded with a raspy lick on her arm.

Will reached over and took one of the flyers from her basket. "What the devil?" he muttered. "You've got to be kidding. You can't go plastering these things all over town."

Erin thought the flyer was striking. After all, she'd written it and designed it herself. In bold orange letters it read:

ASK MAGGIE!
ONLY IN THE *CAPE COD GAZETTE*

Do you have a problem with your love life? Maybe you can't talk to your husband these days. Or perhaps your boyfriend changed the locks and forgot to give you a key. Or he keeps calling you

Michelle even though your name is Doris....

NOW THERE'S HELP!!
WRITE TO MAGGIE, CARE OF THE *GAZETTE*. SHE
HAS NEW AND UNUSUAL ANSWERS FOR YOU.
WRITE TODAY!!!

Will crumpled up the flyer in one hand and tossed
it back in her basket. "What the heck are you trying
to do, ruin Maggie's reputation? This is just lurid
garbage."

Erin squashed her straw hat farther down on her
head. "Of course it's lurid," she snapped. "What did
you expect? Maggie wants to write a lurid column. We
have to promote it so people will know exactly what
we're talking about."

"You should have consulted me on this, Lewis.
Your high-flown *Gazette* is turning into nothing but a
raunchy tabloid."

"How can you call the *Gazette* raunchy when Kendrick's Boat Yard is going to place a full-page ad in the
first issue?"

"No way," Will grumbled. "I never agreed to that,
Lewis. I'm sure not going to advertise in your crazy
paper. Your tactics worry me. From now on I really
am going to follow you. I'm going to stick to you like
gum on your shoe."

"Oh, for goodness' sake. Why don't you just bug
my phone and hire a private detective to hound me?"

Duffy wagged his unruly tail, as if applying for detective duty himself. Will merely smiled again. He
leaned back against a window ledge and fished something from one of his pockets. It looked gruesome, like

the desiccated finger of a cadaver. Erin shuddered, although on closer inspection she realized Will had produced the remnants of a rawhide bone. He tossed it to Duffy, who plunked himself down contentedly on the sidewalk and started gnawing. Both Will and the Scottie seemed to be settling in with Erin on this particular street corner, unmindful of the people who had to push around them. At this time of year the normal population of Jamesport swelled with seasonal visitors and the sidewalks were always busy.

Erin balanced herself on the ledge beside Will, for the moment allowing herself to enjoy his presence. But the enjoyment was short-lived because he started in on her again.

"Too bad I have to begin shadowing you, Lewis," he said in a regretful tone of voice. "But I never know what you're going to do next. Can't have you making deals with Roger Paxton behind my back, that sort of thing."

She glanced sharply at Will. "Thanks to you, the man won't even meet me for a friendly meal. He thinks you and I are involved."

Will's expression was thoughtful. "Where do you imagine he got an idea like that?"

"Look, I think we should clarify this whole ridiculous mess." Erin tugged on the frayed strap of her camera, which was slung crosswise over her shoulder. "It's bad enough being business partners with you, Will. But all this personal stuff is complicating my life no end!"

"So you want to straighten it out," he suggested, sounding much too amenable. "You want to settle once and for all just how uninvolved we are."

He was poking fun at her, making her feel silly. But she wouldn't back down.

"Yes, that's exactly what I want to do. We might as well get everything out in the open and resolve it once and for all."

Will was fishing around in his pockets again. This time he produced a chocolate bar that looked as if it had melted in its wrapper, then hardened again into a contorted shape. "Want some?" he offered.

"Um . . . no thanks."

"You don't know what you're missing." He tore open the wrapper, broke off a chunk of chocolate and popped it into his mouth. "Let's see, where were we— that's right, everything out in the open. I guess that means I can tell you how much I'd like to take you in my arms right now. I'd really kiss you this time, that's what I'd do."

Erin felt the heat blaze in her cheeks, just thinking about the taste of Will's mouth. Today it would be sweetened with the flavor of rich dark chocolate . . .

"All right, so we have this physical thing," she burst out, causing passersby to turn startled faces toward her. "But can't we be reasonable about it for once? Can't you see how much trouble it's causing me?"

He shifted position on the ledge, stretching out his legs in their ragged denim. There was an amused light in his eyes. "I'd like to cause you some more trouble, Erin. Anytime."

"Can't you take this seriously?" she demanded, yanking on her camera strap again. "Things are going too far, Will! We have to stop."

She expected another teasing remark, but suddenly all the joking was gone. The atmosphere between them became strained and uncertain. She and Will stared at each other as the mellow afternoon sun ripened toward dusk.

"I think this is very serious," he said in a quiet voice. "Way too serious. You drive me crazy, Erin. Everything you do annoys the heck out of me—the way you won't listen to me, the way you're always spouting idealistic trash. But I still want to be with you. All the time I want to be with you. It's like someone's beating me over the head with a cast-iron skillet and I keep on asking for more. Believe me, I want to stop the skillet clanging in my ears. I just can't figure out how to do it. I can't figure out how to get you out of my brain!"

CHAPTER EIGHT

A CHILD RAN BY, ponytail flying. Two breathless parents hurried after her, trying to keep up. Other pedestrians jostled past Will and Erin. For a long moment neither one of them spoke. Then Erin dug her fingernails into the flesh of her palms.

"No matter what, we have to stop," she murmured. "What's happening between us . . . none of it makes any sense."

"Not easy to resolve, is it?"

"No."

Will frowned at her. "If I thought taking you to bed would get you off my mind, I'd do it right now. But I'm starting to see that would only make things worse. You'd be an itch under my skin, deeper than ever."

Erin scratched her arm distractedly. "Listen here, Will Kendrick. I'm not going to bed with you. Because I'm not going to fall in love with you and that's final."

"You come up with a good way to end all this and that'll be fine with me, Lewis. But I think about you even when you're not around, damn it. And I'll wager that you think about me."

She couldn't deny that, much as she wanted to. She didn't have any answer for him now. Will chewed morosely on his chocolate bar. Duffy chewed on his rawhide bone. And Erin chewed on the inside of her lip, realizing that bringing things out in the open only made them worse. What existed between her and Will had no simple solution.

"All right," she tried again. "Let's be logical about this. Let's go beyond the emotions and the hormones and all that. First of all, we're not suited for each other in the least. I mean, you have such a skeptical attitude about marriage and you're always ridiculing my ideals. You're not like Ned at all—"

"Lord, you're dredging up the sacred uncle. Do you do that every time you get scared, Erin?" Will stuffed the empty candy-bar wrapper into his pocket, looking her over with an expression of pity. "Every time a man gets too close to you, that's your out—the old Ned routine. No one can possibly live up to your cockeyed image of him, so you're safe a little while longer."

Erin hugged her arms tightly against her body, as if to shield herself from his words. But they stung her anyway, and she had to lash back at him.

"Darn it, I'm not a coward, Will. *You're* the one who breaks out in hives if someone so much as mentions the word marriage!"

They stared at each other, apparently having reached an impasse. Neither one of them said anything more. Then Erin swung onto her bike and started pedaling up a side street, her intention to make a fast getaway from Will. She pumped her legs up and down furiously, spurring the old machine onward. There was only one problem. The bike was so ancient and rusty it barely crept along with each push of the pedals. Meanwhile Will and Duffy strolled along beside her. Even Duffy's stubby legs didn't have any trouble keeping up with the bike.

"I see you're getting a good cardiovascular workout here," Will observed. "That thing you're riding is just as good as a treadmill. Don't let anybody tell you different."

Erin leaned over the handlebars, straining and huffing. The bicycle picked up a few milliseconds of speed, requiring Duffy to trot a little. But Will just walked beside her, thumbs hooked into his belt loops.

Erin struggled for breath, her words coming out in spurts. "Seems to me—there's only one—logical conclusion! I keep out of your way—you keep out of mine. Goodbye, Will." She drew in a deep gulp of air and slammed her foot down on the right pedal. The bike wheezed forward. She hauled down on the left pedal. The bike gave her another inch or so of effort.

Will's breathing hadn't accelerated at all. In fact, he had to slow down his gait so he didn't get ahead of her. "Thinking of entering any races?" he asked in a conversational tone. "You'd be great competition in the Tour de France."

"Why don't you—just get out of here—and leave me alone!" Sweat was starting to drip down Erin's forehead from under her hat. Will looked cool and refreshed.

"You're forgetting our business deal. I told you I was going to protect Maggie's investment at all costs. And that means monitoring everything you do. I don't trust you. I want to know what you're up to next."

"Oh, for crying out loud." She stumbled off her seat and collapsed over the handlebars for a moment. After several gasps for air she started walking her bike, the way she'd been doing most of the afternoon. At least now Will had to lengthen his stride in order to keep up with her.

"It's absurd for you to pursue me all over town," she declared with renewed energy. "All I'm going to do the next few days is look for a story. THE STORY." That was how she thought of it, in capital letters.

"Right off, I don't like the sound of this," Will muttered. "Exactly what story are you talking about?"

"If I knew what story it was, then I wouldn't be having any problems." Erin stopped and knocked the kickstand of the bike into place. She took one of her flyers and slapped it under the windshield wiper of a parked car. "I need one story to make those advertisers pay attention to me. Just one riveting news story. Something major, of course—political corruption or maybe corporate fraud. Something that will have every last person in town reading the *Gazette* and asking for more. Then business owners will be lining up at my office and begging for advertising space in the paper."

Will laughed. "You're wandering around in the clouds again, Lewis. This isn't a big city, and we don't have big stories. Why would we want them, anyway? People come here to get away from crime and corruption."

"Well, crime and corruption sell newspapers," Erin returned. "So that's what I'm looking for. Extortion, fraud, bribery!" She relished the thought of a meaty scandal just waiting to be exposed. But Will was shaking his head as if dumbfounded.

"You're twisted, Erin, really twisted. You talk about high-flown ideals, but then you turn around and act like having felons overrun the town would be the greatest thing in the world for you."

Erin bent down and tugged on a long clump of grass that was growing through a crack in the sidewalk. She wanted to hear the satisfying snap of the grass as she tore it away from the ground. Only it wouldn't budge. She tugged harder, frowning over at Will.

"You distort everything I say," she complained. "No journalist thinks crime is a good thing. But it's the job of a reporter to uncover problems, not ignore them. It's a service to the community. It's a duty, a trust that has to be fulfilled—"

"You're spouting idealistic garbage again. You never lose your talent for that, do you?" Will propped his elbow on top of a whitewashed fence.

Erin gripped both hands around the clump of grass and pulled even harder. The darn stuff wouldn't give, behaving as if it had been cemented into the sidewalk. Duffy padded over and snuffled her hands with interest. Erin heaved backward with all her might. The grass was slippery and she lost her grip on it, landing with a thud on her tailbone.

"Ouch. All right, so I get excited about a decent news story! My blood starts pumping when I find out about kickbacks or investment scams. Is that such a rotten thing? It's what I do for a living. It's what I *could* do for a living, if you'd ever stop badgering me."

Will rubbed his jaw thoughtfully. "Here's a case to illustrate my point. You remember—we were talking about how you drive me crazy but I want to hang around you, anyway. Right now everything you say annoys the heck out of me. You sound like a cross between an ambulance chaser and a crusader. On the other hand, you look mighty good sprawled on the sidewalk like that, your face red as a radish and your hair sticking out all over the place.''

Erin wanted to throttle him. Instead she scrambled to her knees and lunged for that darn clump of grass. This time she went after only one stem, using the theory of divide and conquer. She pulled on it, tugged and yanked. It wouldn't give. She was being defeated by one nefarious strand of grass!

''This isn't natural,'' she said darkly, wishing she had a can of weed killer to brandish as a weapon. ''And it's not natural to be plagued by *you*, Will Kendrick.''

''Face it, Lewis. You're fighting a losing battle.'' He bent down beside her, grabbed half the clump of grass and pulled it out with a good, clean snap.

Erin stared at him and at the grass. ''I don't believe it. There is no justice in this world. None at all!'' She clambered up and grasped the handlebars of her bike, wondering how the following news story would look plastered all over the front page of the *Gazette:* ENRAGED WOMAN ON THREE-SPEED BIKE ATTACKS OBNOXIOUS, INTERFERING MAN. Of course, first she'd have to get the bike in motion, a feat in itself.

''Hey, you're not thinking about running away again, are you?'' Will asked. He came over to her, straddling the front wheel of the old bike and covering her hands with his. The touch of his fingers was warm. He had large and powerful hands, with a bluntness to them, yet they engulfed her own with unexpected tenderness. "I was just about to give you the scoop you're looking for," he said. "The big story in Jamesport."

She wiggled her fingers under his, captivated by his nearness, but struggling to concentrate on the subject of news reporting. "What could you possibly have to tell me? I've already been to the police station and learned all about the number of beer cans littered on the beach last night. I doubt you have anything more scandalous to contribute than that."

He rocked her bike gently back and forth, forcing her to shift her weight. "This thing's got great fenders," he told her. "I wish I had some like this on my car." He gave the bicycle an admiring perusal. Erin suspected he wasn't sincere about the fenders, but she rather liked them herself. They were big and substantial, painted a startling shade of purple that was visible here and there under all the rust.

"You just don't know the right sources for news, Lewis," he went on after a moment. "Don't go to the police station. Captain Sid's Place on Seabell Lane, that's where you'll really hear the town scuttlebutt. Everyone important congregates there for beer and clam chowder."

"Captain Sid's Place?" she asked. "Come on, give me a break. What an absurd name."

"Sid wouldn't appreciate hearing you say that. So he's not a real ship's captain—but who can blame him? The poor guy's terrified to go near the water. Where did you get this bizarre contraption of a bicycle, anyway, steal it from a museum?"

"It's still perfectly serviceable. Just needs a little oil, that's all. It's the bike Uncle Ned let me ride every summer and it means a great deal to me." Erin managed to free one of her hands from Will's hold. She reached over and squeezed the bike's horn. It looked like a small foghorn, actually, and emitted a very satisfying sound like the squawk of a belligerent sea gull. Will jumped a little. Erin instantly felt encouraged and honked a second time, for good measure.

"Go ahead, tell me this great news story of yours. I can hardly wait to hear it."

"Listen, this is the most exciting thing that's happened in a long time. You'd better take it seriously." He paused. "Are you ready?"

"Just tell me!" she groaned.

"All right, this is it. For years there's been a ship's figurehead nailed up over the door of Captain Sid's Place. It's been a good-luck charm for practically the whole town. But one night last week someone stole it. Just like that, someone nabbed Addie Adair. That's what she was called, good old Addie Adair." Will sounded affectionate, as if he was talking about a real person.

Erin tapped her foot impatiently. "That's not news. It sounds like a joke, or a prank of some sort. I need a major story to carry the paper, Will! Something that people really want to hear about."

He looked at her with a mocking expression. "And you call yourself a reporter, Lewis. I'm telling you, the kidnapping of Addie Adair is big news in town. People feel they've lost their good-luck piece, and that's serious business. They want Addie Adair back where she belongs."

For Pete's sake, now he was calling it a kidnapping. Why couldn't there just be a decent political scandal? Erin sighed. Will had mentioned that Captain Sid's Place was a gathering spot for important people. Maybe if she went over there, she'd get a lead on something that was vital and newsworthy—something besides this figurehead snatching. It couldn't hurt, anyway.

"Okay, fine," she said, trying to get rid of Will. "You've been very helpful. Now get out of my way."

He went on straddling her front wheel as if he owned the bike. "Why don't you retire this thing? Even in its good days it was probably a dog." He glanced over at his Scottie. "Nothing personal, McDuff," he added.

"I can take care of my own transportation," Erin said tartly. "Someday this bicycle's going to surprise you. It'll whiz right past you, and then you'll be sorry for all your ridicule."

Will was standing close to her, the wire basket with Maggie's flyers serving as the only barrier between them. His virility seemed especially potent right now as they stood on this deserted little street, the scent of honeysuckle in the air around them and the sky a deep, dusky blue.

If he kissed her, this time she wouldn't give in. She wouldn't let her hormones go rampaging about as before—that was imperative. But even as she made this resolve, Erin felt her knees start to wobble as if Will's lips had already brushed hers.

He looked her over speculatively, his eyes dark and mysterious yet full of humor, too. Then he surprised her by releasing the bike, swinging one leg over the front wheel so he could step away.

"Guess that's about it," he said in a cheerful voice. "See you later, Erin."

It was too easy. She couldn't believe he was going to retreat this conveniently. She gave him some thorough scrutiny; he seemed relaxed and carefree. Aha! That was a suspicious sign, right there. He was up to something.

"What torment are you planning for me now, Will Kendrick? You might as well let me in on it."

He stretched his arms, the gesture implying total lack of concern with her. "Duffy and I want to get on with our walk, that's all. You really must be paranoid, Lewis."

"Hmmph." She still didn't trust him, but decided to make her escape while she could. She tried pedaling the bike once more. But it protested with a horrendous gnashing and screeching of gears, as if she were torturing it. Erin dismounted, trying to have mercy on the bicycle. Ignoring the sound of Will's laughter, she gripped the handlebars and lugged the bike away, back toward Main Street. She glanced over her shoulder at Will and his dog. Will raised his hand in a gesture of farewell. Duffy wagged his scraggly tail a second later, like an echo of his master.

"Disreputable pair," Erin muttered to herself. She began hauling her bike along a circuitous route toward Seabell Lane, looking for Captain Sid's Place. In spite of her evasive maneuvers, she was convinced that any minute she'd see a Scottie peering out at her from a bed of lavender or from a clump of zinnias.

Will Kendrick was too obstinate a man to give her any genuine freedom.

It was slow going, but Erin refused to place any blame on her old bike. As soon as she had the *Gazette* under way, she'd take some time and spruce up the bicycle, pamper it with a new chain and some spiffy tires. She didn't know where Uncle Ned had unearthed the bike; even back in her childhood summers the thing had been a wreck. But Erin would never forget the day she'd first seen it, a big yellow bow tied to the handlebars, Uncle Ned grinning as he wheeled it over to her. The memory was a special one, like so many of the memories Ned had given her. Erin felt heartened by it, and continued her meandering route through town. She traveled up and down several streets until she was finally convinced she wasn't being pursued by the Kendricks.

At last she arrived at Captain Sid's, and found it to be a shabby wooden building tucked away between more respectable neighbors. The paint on its clapboards was a pale green, the color of sick seaweed, and much of it was peeling away. A darker blotch of green above the door marked the missing figurehead's former resting spot.

Erin scanned the place without much hope; it didn't look promising at all. Then a tall figure materialized from the shadows at the side of the building. It looked menacing in the early twilight, until a smaller figure jumped out from the shadows and let out a gruff but friendly bark. None other than Will Kendrick and his shaggy cohort.

"I knew it," Erin exclaimed. "I knew you couldn't leave me alone. You've stooped so low that now you're lurking in alleys!"

"It's just that you've inspired me, Lewis. After listening to you talk, I've decided maybe I should become an investigative reporter myself. I feel it's almost an obligation on my part. What did you call it? A sacred trust, that's it." He looked pleased with himself and his humor.

"Oh, shut up," Erin said. But nothing seemed capable of stopping him. Here he was, wrestling her bike away from her and stashing it in the very alley where he'd been lurking.

"Wait a minute!" she protested. "Someone might steal it there. After all, someone grabbed this Addie Adair of yours right from over the door."

"Rest easy, Lewis. No one—and I mean no one—is going to steal the purple wonder from you. Not even if you put a sign on it advertising for thieves. Come on, we have to get inside before there's a run on the chowder." He took her arm and propelled her up the steps and into Captain Sid's. Duffy followed close at their heels, as if determined not to be left out of anything.

Inside, the air was dim and smoky, smelling strongly of fried fish. Captain Sid had made at least a cursory attempt at interior decoration. Fishing nets tangled with strings of seashells were draped on a few of the walls, and a crude painting of a Nantucket whaleboat hung crookedly against another wall. But apparently Sid had lost interest after these attempts; his vague seafaring motif petered out to include only a few pieces of driftwood propped up in a corner here and there.

The place was noisy and crowded, most of the tables filled with people. Will shouldered a path to the bar, still towing Erin. She found herself deposited on a stool in front of the bar, which was a long, impressive slab of weathered wood. Will claimed a stool beside her and Duffy staked out an area right at her feet. Once again the Kendricks were taking her over, drawing her in to be part of a peculiar trio.

"Lewis, this is Captain Sid himself," Will announced in her ear, making her start. "And, Sid, this is Erin Lewis, who's going to investigate the abduction of Addie Adair."

On the other side of the bar a small man was methodically pumping beer into mugs. He had bushy gray eyebrows and the bald spot on his skull was surrounded by a curling gray fringe of hair. The long shape of his face was emphasized by an expression of acute mournfulness. He looked like a pessimistic philosopher. After setting two mugs of beer in front of Will and Erin, he reached over and shook her hand with surprising firmness. His thin fingers were so strong that their grip made her knuckles crack. She rubbed her hand after he released it.

"No one's been able to find Addie Adair," he remarked sorrowfully. "She was my inspiration. I owe all the good fortune in my life to her. Nothing is the same without her. I feel like I've lost my best friend."

Erin studied Captain Sid, wondering if he could possibly be serious about all this. Then she glanced at Will. Were the two men pulling her leg in some ridiculous prank? But Will was nursing his beer with a respectful look on his face, as if Sid was discussing a recently deceased loved one. And Captain Sid himself went on speaking with a solemn demeanor.

"Miss Lewis, Addie presided over my door for twenty-five years." He sighed. "I can see her now, lifting her skirts like she didn't give a sniff what anybody thought about her. But now she's gone. All gone."

Will nudged Erin. "Aren't you going to write any of this down?" he asked. "What kind of reporter are you, anyway?"

"I'll spell the names for you," Captain Sid offered, his long face beginning to look slightly less glum. "Addie's full name was Adeline. A-d-e-l-i-n-e. Adeline Adair."

Next, Sid would probably begin describing Addie's height and weight, along with any distinguishing scars or tattoos. Erin wanted to put her head down on her arms and laugh. Or cry. Instead she took her pencil and notepad from the back pocket of her shorts and obligingly flipped to a clean page. Maybe if she went along with this farce, she could still get a lead on some important news.

"All right," she began. "When exactly did the kidnapping—I mean, the theft—take place?"

"Week ago, Thursday night," Sid answered. "Had to be in the middle of the night when she was taken. I came by real early Friday morning and she wasn't there. I always come by early on Friday to start an extra batch of chowder."

"Hey, Sid, give the lady some of your famous chowder, then," Will broke in. "Give me a bowl, too.

The loss of Addie Adair is not a subject for an empty stomach.''

A moment later Erin was faced with a steaming bowl of clam chowder that she hadn't asked for. She wasn't even hungry. Confound Will Kendrick!

"Go ahead, taste it," he urged, a big spoonful of the chowder disappearing into his mouth. "You don't know what life is all about until you've experienced Sid's chowder."

"I thought life was all about sailing and nothing else," Erin retorted.

"That, too. Sailing and Sid's chowder. And Addie Adair. You don't need much else. But it looks like you need some help getting into the spirit of things. Open wide."

Before she could stop him, he'd taken her spoon and dipped it into her bowl.

"What the heck—" she protested, but that was a mistake. The minute she started to speak, Will popped the spoon into her mouth. He was so enthusiastic that she nearly choked. When she recovered, she realized this was the best chowder she'd ever tasted. It was rich and creamy, with savory bits of salt pork and just the right hint of onion.

"Oh, my," she murmured.

"I told you it was good." Will started dipping her spoon into her bowl again. She grabbed the spoon and glared at him.

"I think I can manage this job on my own."

His eyes shone with amusement. "I'm not so sure about that, Lewis. Seems to me you need my help with everything, even when it's a simple matter of clam chowder."

Erin frowned at him, but she took some of the oyster crackers he offered her. They sat side by side, enjoying Captain Sid's delicious food. Somehow Duffy had ended up with his own bowl of chowder and was slurping away happily at Erin's feet. Altogether it was a very cozy atmosphere.

Erin set her spoon down with a clatter, wondering what was happening to her. She seemed to be forgetting about her need for a big news story. Instead she was becoming very interested in the fate of Addie Adair. She was happy and relaxed, completely the opposite of the way she'd been at the elegant Bayberry Inn.

Will was smiling at her as if he knew exactly what she was feeling. He reached over and took her hand in his. Before she could analyze what she was doing, she gave his fingers an answering squeeze. They were sharing something warm and companionable. They even seemed to belong here together at Captain Sid's.

It was so comfortable to be with Will like this. But it was also terrifying. For the first time Erin was admitting that she and Will Kendrick might actually belong together. And if she started thinking like that . . . what on earth would happen to her next?

CHAPTER NINE

THERE WAS NO LONGER a teasing light in Will's eyes. He gazed at Erin with an intensity that shook her, his fingers tightening on hers. Around them eddied the noise and smoky air of Captain Sid's Place, but Erin was locked in her own private world with Will. Her breath came unevenly as she stared back at him, and she was aware of the pounding of her heart. It was like a pulse joining her to him. She couldn't seem to speak or move. All she could do was sit there and take in every detail of him with longing—his dark hair tousled over his forehead, the deep brown of his eyes, the sensual, expressive lines of his mouth, his scent of clean sweat and sea spray.

She was starting to belong to him, right now, right here, even as she struggled to keep herself intact. With Will she was feeling emotions more intense than any she'd ever imagined. She was afraid.

He leaned toward her with urgency. "Erin," he began. "Erin, I—"

"Say, Will," interrupted one of the many voices around them. "Guess who's sitting over there? It's Jonas. Gone in his beer, he is."

Will rubbed a hand over his forehead like a man coming out of a dream. He stared at Erin a moment longer, but he didn't finish what he'd been about to say. With a curt shrug he slid off his bar stool and left her.

Erin felt relieved, yet at the same time oddly bereft. She was still intact; she hadn't given too much to Will, after all. For a time at least she could breathe easily again. But she sensed that she'd missed something vital and essential just now, as if a beautiful piece of scenery had flashed by outside her field of vision. What had Will meant to say to her? She'd never know...because she couldn't risk asking him about it.

Erin bent down to give Duffy the rest of the crackers, then turned to see where Will was going. He'd reached a table across from the bar, where an old man sat hunched over a mug of beer. Erin recognized the man immediately; he was the nasty old guy who'd been tending Will's tackle shop that first day.

"How long have you been here, Jonas?" Will asked in a beleaguered voice. "What about the boat yard?"

The old man didn't seem perturbed. "Don't worry about it. I decided to close up early today. No one wants to rent your boats anyway, William." He cackled into his beer.

Erin knew the old man's words weren't true at all. Will was popular in Jamesport. His easy charm drew people naturally to him—not to mention the fact that he had a reputation for providing superb seaworthy sailboats.

Will, however, seemed resigned to this sort of comment from Jonas. He came back to sit beside Erin, grumbling under his breath. There was now an awkward constraint between them.

"Sounds like you ought to be supervising Jonas, not hounding me," she told him.

He frowned at her. "Jonas manages the place just fine when I'm gone. So he left a little early today. Everybody's entitled to some time off."

"I wonder which one of you is the boss," Erin remarked.

"I don't need to be his boss. Jonas is more like a partner. A friend. That's the way it should be." Will seemed defensive about the old man, as if determined to guard him from attack. Erin was reluctantly attracted by this protectiveness of Will's.

"So... how long has Jonas worked for you?" she asked. "Or with you—whichever it is."

"Years," was his terse reply. Then someone slapped Will on the shoulder and started talking to him. Erin was left to sip her beer. She'd glimpsed in Will a stubborn loyalty to Jonas, much like his devotion toward his Aunt Maggie. It was clear that he'd fight to protect his own. Erin wondered how it would be if she actually did belong to him. What would it be like to have him fighting for her instead of against her? She gripped her mug with both hands, trying not to envy Maggie and Jonas.

"I say it's a conspiracy," intoned a contralto voice behind Erin. "Some organized group is obviously behind the disappearance of Addie Adair. Who knows where they'll strike next?"

"I think it was an act of political protest," answered another voice, this one thick and nasal as if its owner was suffering from a summer cold. "That's my bet, a misguided act of protest. Achoo!" sneezed the voice.

Everyone had something to say about the mystery of Addie Adair. Everyone, that was, except for Jonas.

The old man sat hunched alone without uttering a word. His arms were resting on the table in front of him, his head lowered. He reminded Erin of a Cape Cod scrub tree, gnarled and bent from the onslaught of ocean winds but able to root deep in the sand. His silence was intent, as if he wanted to make sure he heard everything said around him even though he wasn't joining in.

He was a part of Will's life...an important part, it seemed. Erin's natural curiosity was aroused, along with a poignant yearning. She couldn't help herself. She wanted to know more about Will. In fact, she wanted to know everything about him.

She glanced at Will. He was deep in conversation, ardently defending a baseball team that had just lost six games in a row. Loyalty again! She sat beside him a moment longer, then looked at Jonas. The old man was a link to Will and because of that he drew Erin.

With a decisive gesture she took up her mug and headed over to his table. She pulled out a chair next to him and sat down. The look in his rheumy eyes wasn't welcoming, but she didn't let that stop her.

"What's your opinion about Addie Adair?" she asked. "Who do you think took her?"

"Don't know. Don't care. Go away, missie, and do your newspaper nosing somewhere else. You're as big a nuisance as your uncle. That old codger Ned."

"Takes one old codger to know another," Erin retorted. Because of Jonas's crusty manner, she didn't feel the need for false politeness.

He gave a raspy cackle of a laugh. "You're as ornery as Ned, too. Now leave me be."

Erin propped her elbows on the table. It was rickety, with one leg shorter than the others, and it tipped under the pressure of her weight. She was caught by surprise, but Jonas's body moved easily with the shifting of the table. He might have been an extension of the wood surface himself, a carving of a grizzled old man.

Erin leaned back and observed him. His hair was a salt-and-pepper stubble scattered over his knobby pate; his nose was large and bulbous and red-veined. Much of his skin was mottled and bumpy, so he really did look like some hardy, tuberous growth molded onto the chair. He wasn't a stunning specimen of humanity, but Erin was fascinated by him because he possessed Will's loyalty and friendship.

"What are you looking at?" Jonas demanded.

Erin lifted her shoulders. "I'm interested in you because Will appears to care about you. I can't figure out why. My first impression of you is that you're not exactly lovable." She found it easy to be straight with Jonas; she suspected he was the type of person who'd be offended by anything less than total honesty. Now he gave her a grimace that was almost a smile.

"William's been hankering after you, missie. No explaining that, either."

She smiled back at him. "Fair enough. Maybe Will just has strange taste in people." She took off her camera and placed it in front of her. Then she propped her elbows on the table again, carefully this time. But Jonas took hold of the table edge and started jiggling it as if to dislodge Erin from her place. She could tell she was a nuisance to him, like a barnacle on a ship's hull—an annoyance to be dispatched, nothing more.

That didn't bother her. She liked the fact that Jonas didn't have any veneer of civility. She could talk and act frankly with him because he made no pretense of liking her.

Erin held onto the table as it rocked back and forth on its crooked legs. There was a malevolent look on Jonas's face as he jiggled the table harder, his hands like two knotted roots clamped onto the edge. The beer mugs jounced around and Erin's camera started to clatter about, too. Then abruptly Jonas let go and the table gave one last bounce. Erin grabbed her camera just as it went sliding off toward the floor.

Jonas stuck his finger into a puddle of beer that had sloshed over the rim of his mug. "Seems you want something from me," he said. "Guess you won't go away till you get it."

Erin made sure her lens cap was still on tight. Fortunately her camera was a sturdy one and had seen a lot worse abuse than this over the years. "I want you to tell me about Will," she answered. "Just little things like why he puts up with you and whether or not he drinks milk in his coffee. Simple details like that."

"Black coffee," grated the old man. "What do you take William for, a weak-livered ninny? No milk! Now I've told you. Go away."

"You still haven't explained why he tolerates someone as sour and nasty as you," Erin persisted. "I find that very intriguing."

Jonas gave a dry hacking cough that made him sound as if he was stuffed full of autumn leaves. Then he took a long swallow of beer. "Anybody will tell you about me and William's grandpa. We fished together. Partners." Jonas was silent for a while, then went on.

"William used to wait for us on the wharf with his grandma. Funny kid, curly hair dangling over his ears. Only the ocean for him. Bawled his head off whenever he couldn't go out in the boat with us." Now Jonas clamped his mouth shut, as if jealous of his memories and unwilling to let any more of them escape for Erin's benefit. But he'd already given something to her, an image of Will as a child. She turned it over in her mind, examining it and enjoying it.

Jonas shifted in his chair, his joints creaking a little. "I know what you're really sniffing after, missie. A story about Addie for your dang newspaper. That's what you want. But you won't get it from me."

Something in his tone alerted Erin's instincts. Something about the offhand but affectionate way he'd let the word "Addie" slip out.

"Sure, I'm looking for a news story," she admitted. "But not just any story. It has to be something people will really want to read. Right now all I have is this Addie Adair hoopla. Not much to get excited about."

As if to confirm her words, Jonas sank lower in his chair, his body settling into immobility like a chunk of sediment. He yawned with a patent display of boredom, exposing a full set of yellowed teeth. But he was too deliberate in his efforts. Erin's investigative antennae were quivering at full alert now.

"I suppose I could make a good human-interest story out of Addie," she murmured, speaking as if to herself. "That would be something, anyway. People really seem interested in what happened to her. Everyone except you, of course. You're acting like you don't give a darn if she sank into the ocean and will never be seen again."

Jonas's eyelids had drifted downward. He gave the impression of being sound asleep, complete with a rumbling snore. But Erin suspected he was still listening to her. She leaned forward, rocking the table to remind him of her presence. He snored a little louder.

"You know, somehow I just don't buy it," she said. "Your lack of interest in Addie Adair. You're going to way too much trouble to make me think you don't care. But you've been sitting here like you want to hear what everyone else thinks. I have a hunch you know something about her disappearance. It's just a hunch, but there it is."

She paused to see if her words would have any effect. After quite a prolonged moment one of the old man's eyelids popped open. A single bloodshot eye stared at her.

"What if I did know something?" he asked. "Not saying I do—but what if I did?"

A familiar thrill of triumph went through Erin. Whenever one of her hunches promised to pan out like this, her adrenaline started pumping. She felt good, as if she'd been out running and stirring up her blood. All right, so maybe she still hoped for a big story. But right now she had the mystery of Addie Adair to work with and she was getting swept up by it. She jiggled the table again.

"Like I told you, I think I can make a human-interest story out of Addie. Of course, I'd need to know what happened to her. That'll make people read the *Gazette.* If you do know something and you tell me about it . . . well, you'll be part of the news. Unless you want to remain anonymous. Maybe we can arrange something that will make both of us happy.''

He opened his other bleary eye. ''I'm not saying I know anything. Too dang much fuss going on already.''

''Fuss is news,'' Erin remarked, ''no matter what it's about. That's just the way it is.'' She sat back and waited, for the next move belonged to Jonas. She wouldn't try to manipulate or coerce him. Tactics like that probably wouldn't succeed with him, anyway— and she'd always believed that straightforwardness was her best tool as a reporter.

He hunched still further over his mug. He was either deep in thought or contemplating his next swig of beer. Erin wiped at the moisture that had beaded on the outside of her own mug. She continued to wait.

At last Jonas lifted his head. No emotion was betrayed on his mottled, stubbly face. ''Maybe I have something to tell you. Maybe not. You come to the boat yard tonight around ten. Bring William with you, but nobody else. Think you can handle that, missie?''

Erin nodded calmly, even though she was elated. ''I'll be there.''

He stood up with a creaking of bones, his joints sounding stiff and unused. Now that he was standing, his rounded shoulders made him seem vulnerable. He swayed for a second as if unsure of his balance, and Erin started to reach out a hand to him. But he grunted with ill temper and she stayed herself. It was obvious that Jonas would accept no sympathy or help from her. He gripped the edge of the table and gave it one last jerk. Erin had to grab her camera again.

Jonas shuffled away. As he passed the bar, he gave Will a poke in the back that could hardly be called a gesture of affection. For a moment it seemed Will would reach out to help steady Jonas—but then, like Erin, he withdrew his hand. With a worried expression, he watched the old man weave unsteadily to the door.

Erin sipped her beer. Even after Jonas disappeared, it seemed to her that his wheezing cackle echoed above the noise of the bar, like the laughter of some malevolent spirit.

"LORD, I TURN MY BACK on you for one minute and the next thing I know you're arranging devious meetings at my boat yard in the middle of the night. First Maggie, and now Jonas. When will you stop messing with the people in my life?" Will sounded angry as he strode alongside Erin in the dark, his hand gripping her elbow. She tried to shake him off.

"Jonas is the one who set up this appointment," she declared. "I didn't force him into anything."

"Dammit, Erin. He's an old man, and not a very strong one. The doctor says his heart could go any time. We had a bad scare only a few months ago—we thought Jonas was on his way out for sure. What the hell do you think you're doing, churning him up like this?"

"Look, all we had was a little chat. Almost a friendly chat, in a perverse sort of way. I believe Jonas and I understand each other very well. I can tell you he doesn't want to be treated like an invalid."

Will tightened his grip on her elbow. "You don't understand anything, Lewis. The only reason I'm letting Jonas work at the boat yard is because he needs to feel useful. Otherwise I'd have him flat on his back in bed, resting the way the doctor told him to do. And I wouldn't let him talk to rattlebrained reporters like you. I still don't know if I'm going to allow this asinine meeting tonight. What could Jonas have to tell you about Addie Adair, anyway?"

Erin hurried on down the street, pulling Will with her. "You're so darn overprotective of people," she complained. "Jonas can decide for himself who he wants to talk to and what he wants to say. Give him that much dignity, at least."

"I respect his independence more than anyone. But that doesn't mean I have to let you go rampaging into his life!"

Will was definitely too protective of those he loved. That was an endearing quality as well as an infuriating one. If he ever did fall in love with a woman, he'd surely give her all the loyalty and constancy that were in his nature.

Erin walked even faster. The ocean air was fresh, with a hint of chill. Summer nights on the Cape were usually cool like this. Erin had changed into corduroy jeans and a long-sleeved cotton shirt, allowing her hair to flow free without a hat. But she still carried her camera slung over one shoulder, ready in case she needed it. No matter what Will Kendrick thought of her, she was a journalist in her heart and soul. She couldn't let him stop her from doing her job.

Lights glimmered on the water of the harbor, like stars that had fallen and melted into the ocean. The humid taste of salt was in the air and a dampness clung to Erin's skin. They had reached the boat yard now, the three of them—for Duffy had padded along behind Erin and Will, a small dark shape in the darker night. All was deserted, no sign of life except for a single lamp glowing in a second-story window of the tackle shop.

"That's where Jonas is," Will said, motioning his head toward the lighted window. "He lives up there. But we're not going to see him yet. I still haven't decided if I'll let you bother him again." With that, Will paced restlessly out onto the dock.

Erin followed close behind him, her hands clenched in frustration. "You're the one who got me started on this story," she reminded him.

"That's not the point."

"Well, confound you, what *is* the point?" She stood in front of him, challenging him, her head tilted back. His face was shadowed in the moonlight, some lines harsh yet others softened. She gazed up at him, trying to read his expression. He was mysterious to her.

"There's no winning with you, Erin . . . no winning with myself." His voice was low and rough as he pulled her toward him.

She didn't resist. Instead she went into his arms freely, with an ache that demanded to be satisfied. For an instant her camera pressed awkwardly between their bodies, but then she dropped it by its strap onto the planks at her feet. Now there was nothing to keep her away from him. She slipped her hands up around his shoulders, delighting in the ripple of muscles under her fingers. At first his lips were cool against hers, as cool as the night air. But gradually the kiss grew heated. Erin's desire flared like the stars reflected in the ocean. She'd longed for ease of the ache inside her, but it was actually deepening under Will's touch. She needed more of him, always more...

With a small moan she broke off the kiss, pressing her face hard against his chest. She was appalled at the tears scalding her eyes. Before she could stop herself, she was weeping silently against Will's T-shirt.

"Erin, what's wrong? Tell me." Now his voice was tender and that truly undid her. Her sobs came in hiccups. He patted her gently on the back, over and over. Then his hands tangled in her hair, cradling her head even closer to him. "Tell me what it is, Erin. What's hurting you?"

She blotted her face on his T-shirt, drawing breath in with ragged gasps. "It's you," she managed to get out, her voice muffled against his chest. "It's the way you make me feel...you make me feel too much." She lifted her head and looked at him again in the moonlit night. Now that she'd started, she was eager to get everything out.

"Will, you scare me. Every emotion you make me experience—anger, happiness, desire—it's magnified a hundred times over. I can't live this way. It'll tear me apart." Her words tumbled to a halt. And Will went on holding her, smoothing her hair and patting her back.

"Erin, you know you've been driving me crazy, too. Maybe we should just give in to it—whatever's happening between us."

She pulled away from his embrace. "There's no hope of a relationship between you and me, Will. We don't care about the same things in life. We don't have the same ideals—and no matter what you say, ideals are important! I want to change the world at least a little, and all you want to do is sail around it in a boat. You're mired in your own complacency. You're too damn satisfied with life.''

Will kicked a coil of rope with his sneakered foot, muttering an oath. But when he spoke next, his voice was quiet. ''I know what you're trying to do here, Erin. You're so frightened of what you feel for me that you're pushing me away with words—with your visions and dreams that don't have any substance at all.''

Erin turned and strode back along the dock. ''Maybe I'm smart, pushing you away! Because you really don't have any respect for who I am or what I believe. We can't build a relationship on that.''

Will kept pace with her. ''Go ahead, make some more excuses. Then you won't need the courage to say you love me.''

Erin brought herself up short. She took a deep breath. ''Can you say it to *me?*'' she asked. ''Can you honestly say that you love me?''

CHAPTER TEN

WILL STARED AT ERIN with an expression that in the darkness she couldn't read. "I'd have to be off my head to be in love with you, Lewis!"

"Well, then." Deciding that she'd achieved a victory, however warped, Erin marched up to the tackle shop. "I'm going to talk to Jonas. You can come with me or not, as you please."

There was an odd bumping noise behind her. Wondering what new tactic Will might be using, she swiveled around. Only it wasn't Will. It was Duffy, dragging her camera along with the strap clamped in his teeth.

She bent down to give him a quick pat behind the ears and to rescue her camera. When Duffy gave her an affectionate lick in return, she almost started crying all over again. The Kendricks definitely had a watery effect on her and she didn't like that at all. She was upset, unsettled and just plain discombobulated. She didn't know how to set herself to rights again.

A narrow outside staircase led up to the second story of the tackle shop. Erin began climbing the steps, followed by Will. He was in a mood foul enough to match her own.

"No one listens to me, dammit," he griped. "I told Jonas I didn't want him to strain his heart going up and down these stairs. I told him to move into my house. But did he pay any attention to me? No. Does Maggie pay any attention when I talk to her? Do you, Lewis? Hell, no."

They reached a small balcony and Will banged a fist against the railing as if to test its strength.

"Nobody listens," he bellowed. "I can't control a single one of you. What's happening to my life?"

"If obedience is what you want, you'll just have to depend on Duffy." The Scottie had remained below at Will's command.

"Hah! You'd be surprised what the dog gets up to behind my back. No, the whole lot of you is conspiring against me." He rapped on the door to Jonas's apartment with much greater force than necessary.

"Come in, already," called the old man in his raspy voice. "You're late!"

Will opened the door and with a minimum of politeness ushered Erin inside. She'd expected disorder, but instead found an incredible tidiness in Jonas's living quarters. The furniture was simple, but there were no rickety tables here. Wooden surfaces gleamed in the lamplight, unmarred by even a speck of sand or dust. Books were lined up on their shelves in regimental order, and several rows of mugs on the kitchen counter were equally rigid. Jonas obviously ruled his domain with a despotic hand. Erin wiped her feet twice on the doormat, concerned that she might track in a smidgen of dirt and thus incur the old man's wrath.

He was hunched in a rocker, bony knees poking up at two different angles. "Sit down," he ordered. "Maybe we'll talk. Then again, maybe we won't."

Now that she was intruding on his territory, Erin felt at a disadvantage with Jonas. But she knew the best thing to do was go along with whatever he wanted; if she was patient enough she'd get results from him. She settled herself in a straight-backed chair, Will taking a seat across from her.

Jonas rocked in his rocker without saying another word. Back and forth, back and forth. Will scowled at Erin. She scowled at Will. It was mesmerizing to stare into his dark eyes for such a long period of time. Erin glanced around the small apartment, looking for something else to focus on.

What struck her most was the lack of personal things in the room. Usually people surrounded themselves with a clutter of telling details—photographs of loved ones, cards received in the mail, a jigsaw puzzle or the accoutrements of some hobby. But with Jonas order and anonymity prevailed, as if he was determined to win the ultimate battle against chaos. Erin looked at the mugs lined up on the kitchen counter. There were quite a few of them in different colors and designs. It was a relief to see some spark of individuality in the apartment, after all. She wondered if that was Jonas's hobby, collecting mugs.

"Jonas, enough of this," Will said. "I can tell you're getting all worked up about something. If you don't want to talk, fine. But go to bed. Get some rest."

"I don't need a nursemaid. And I've been thinking this matter through. It's time to do something about Addie Adair. That's not her real name. Never was her real name."

Erin leaned forward. "So you know what happened to her! Don't you, Jonas?"

"'Course I know." He gave one of his dry cackles. "I'm not a fool. Nothing could happen to her without me knowing about it. I promised I'd take care of her, and I have." With a great deal of creaking and wheezing, Jonas struggled up from his rocker. He shuffled into his bedroom, then turned and poked his head back through the doorway. "Come on! What's keeping the both of you?"

Will and Erin reached the door at the same time. They jostled each other awkwardly.

"Hang it all, let me by," Erin said. They ended up squeezing through together, both of them grumbling.

Neatness reigned in this room, also. The counterpane on the bed was smoothed out with a taut precision that would have made a drill sergeant happy. But the room was dominated by a large canvas-covered lump against one wall. Jonas tugged gently at the canvas, pulling it away.

Will and Erin stared. And Will shook his head in wonder.

"I don't believe it," he said. "It's Addie Adair."

She was beautiful, even propped there awkwardly against the wall instead of gracing the prow of a ship. Addie Adair lifted her wooden skirt and grinned as if the world had been created as a gift especially for her. The low-cut bodice of her dress revealed her to be pleasantly buxom. Although the black paint of her hair was chipping off, coquettish ringlets and curls softened her face. She seemed impudent, feminine and strong-minded all at once. A strong woman, Addie Adair. That was Erin's conclusion right away.

Jonas spoke to Addie, his voice as raspy as sand-paper. "There, girl. There. It's the best thing, what's happening now. You know it is."

Will sat down heavily on the edge of the bed, the springs squeaking in protest under his weight. "Well, Jonas. I guess you can still surprise me. How'd she get here?"

The old man scratched his nose. "Never mind about that. Job's done. That's all you need to know."

Will groaned. "Are you going to tell us why she's here?"

"If you'd quit jabbering, William." Jonas lowered himself into an armchair beside Addie. He reached out and put his hand on her shoulder, where her bright blue dress had slipped down in risqué fashion. "First thing you need to know is that her name isn't Addie. It's Luisa Coelho." He made the name sound like po-etry, even as he grated it through the rusty filter of his voice. "Don't know who started to call her Addie Adair. But that was fine with me. Never wanted any-body to know who she really was."

Erin sat down cross-legged on the floor, pulling out her pencil and notepad. She began to write as Jonas went on speaking.

"Luisa Coelho. She was a friend of your grand-ma's, William. Luisa and Marianna, two of the pret-tiest girls in Jamesport. Your grandma was already married back then, but Luisa was younger. A lot of fellows were after her. You know which one she picked? She picked me." Jonas sounded proud. And his voice wasn't quite so scratchy anymore, as if talk-ing about Luisa had loosened up his vocal cords.

"Kept company with Luisa for a year. But that spring a big nor'easter blew up. Her father's barge ran aground on a shoal. Off Monomoy Point, that's where it happened. Luisa was with her dad. Never found the bodies."

Erin's pencil stilled on her notepad. She looked at Jonas and saw that he'd tightened his hand on Addie Adair's shoulder.

"Used to have nightmares about it," he said. "Sometimes still do. See the waves breaking over the side of the barge and the fog too thick. Luisa and her dad swept into the ocean..." Jonas was silent for a long moment. Then he stirred himself, clearing his throat with a gruff sound.

"Problem was, before she met me Luisa took up with one of those dang artist fellows used to spend the summer here. Statue maker, he was. Said he wanted to make a statue of Luisa. Said she belonged on a ship. So he carved Addie Adair here. Looks just like Luisa, every bit."

Erin gazed at Addie Adair. Or rather at Luisa, whose lively brown eyes were opened wide as if to take in every sight offered to her. And no petite button nose for Luisa; she possessed a good solid nose. The artist had done such a wonderful job that he left Erin longing to know the real woman. Surely Luisa Coelho shouldn't have died young. She should have grown old with Jonas, bringing warmth and life to his rigid surroundings.

Jonas shifted in his chair. "Luisa always did hanker for adventure. Planned to run away with this statue maker. Planned to, anyway, till she found him with his suspenders down in Miriam Gardner's front parlor. Luisa told him right then what to do with his statue. She settled for me after that. Said she'd marry a fisherman any day." Jonas gave a cackle. His gnarled hand stroked Addie's shoulder.

"The statue maker left town. Thrown out on his ear by Miriam Gardner's three brothers, that's how he left. But Luisa started to worry about the figurehead he'd carved. Anyone saw it, they'd know it was Luisa for sure. Too much of her showing altogether. Could've been a big scandal." He glanced sideways at Addie Adair's buxom outline. Her wooden curves were emphasized by the low-cut dress slipping down off both her shoulders. Jonas glanced quickly away again, as if he didn't want to embarrass Addie. He struggled out of his armchair and began shuffling about the room.

"I promised Luisa I'd find the figurehead, make sure nothing happened to her reputation. Only I didn't know where the artist fellow had gone. Didn't know what he did with the carving. Then Luisa died."

Will stood up from the bed. "Jonas, you don't need to talk anymore. We've heard enough. You should get some sleep now."

The old man swatted his hand impatiently at Will. "Don't mollycoddle me, William. Can't stand it when you do that to me. Whole story's got to come out. I kept looking for that figurehead, years after Luisa was gone. Never could find a clue. Till one day she shows up over Sid's doorway. My Luisa, out there for every-body to see. Sid wouldn't let her go, either. Said he'd bought her at an auction in Eastham and how it'd be bad luck to take her down once she was up there over his door. Couldn't bargain with him. So there she stayed. Some folks said she looked familiar, and that old cow Miriam Gardner used to come down to Sid's Place just so she could smirk at my Luisa. It was a bad time, William. Bad.''

Will rubbed the back of his neck, looking both sorrowful and perplexed. ''Heck, Jonas, if I'd known about this, maybe I could've done something to help.''

''You were ten years old when Sid got Luisa. What were you going to do?'' Jonas growled. ''Your grandpa and your grandma, they said it was best not to kick up a fuss. Just leave Sid be, and let Luisa have her place over his door. So that's what I did. Pretty soon folks started calling her Addie. Miriam Gardner went to live with her daughter in Connecticut, and after that no one knew Addie was really Luisa. I kept watch over her all these years. Kept her secret safe. Till I had that scare couple months ago and thought I was a goner. Knew I had to take care of Addie before I died.''

Jonas creaked his way back to Addie Adair, placing a hand on her head as if about to give her a blessing. ''I'm ready to die—not afraid of it, soon as I take care of Addie. When I'm gone, can't have her up there for show over Sid's door. Time's come for her to have the proper resting place. Always bothered me Luisa didn't have a body in her grave. But now she's going to have a proper headstone. A figurehead, that is, topside of her grave. That's what I plan for her.'' After this announcement his reedy voice faded away like an old phonograph recording.

Erin bent over her pad, intently jotting down more notes. But she was interrupted when Will crossed the room to jab a finger at her.

"All right, that's enough, Lewis. You can stop. Not a word said here is going to show up in the *Gazette*. You got that?"

From her position on the floor she glared at Will's jean-clad knees. "What I print in the newspaper isn't up to you, Will Kendrick. Jonas asked me to come here tonight and listen to his story."

"And what do you think will happen if it goes public?" Will demanded. "Jonas has committed a theft. He could go to jail. Is that what you want?"

Erin scrambled to her feet so she wouldn't be at such a disadvantage. "Of course I don't want him to go to jail. But Jonas knew what he was doing when he took Addie Adair. I'm sure he's ready to face up to the full responsibility of his actions."

Will jabbed his finger at her again, almost poking her in the sternum. "Dammit, all you want is news for your blasted newspaper. You don't care about Jonas at all."

"That's not true!" she protested. "I do care. And I care about Luisa Coelho, too. I want to write this story so other people will understand how much it matters that Jonas and Luisa loved each other." She gripped her notepad, wrinkling the pages in her fervor. "Don't you see, Will? This story has to be told. It's begging to be told! And I'm the one who has to tell it."

Will stepped closer to her. "You're not only pig-headed, Lewis, you're arrogant. You don't own anything Jonas has said, and you're not going to print a word of it."

"Stop yammering, the two of you." Jonas interposed himself between Erin and Will, prodding them apart with his knobby hands. Erin caught a whiff of garlic emanating from the old man, along with another pungent odor like the smell of mulched tea bags. "This is the way it is," Jonas said in a commanding tone. "All these years I've been trying to hide the truth about my Luisa and that statue maker. Maybe that's what she would've wanted from me. Tried to do my best. But no reason Luisa should've been ashamed of herself. Just liked a little excitement in her life, that's all. And now I got one chance to put her to rest. If I try to sneak her into the cemetery, won't do me any good. Next morning Sid'll be dragging her back to hang over his door."

Will was looking more and more cantankerous, but he made an obvious effort to sound reasonable. "Look, this is what we'll do, Jonas. You and I will go talk to Sid in private. Right now, if that's what you want. We'll work something out with him—no need to involve the whole town. Sid's a fair man. I'm sure we can come to terms with him."

Jonas gave an expressive snort. "Sid's a beefwit, that's what he is. Won't go outside without checking his dang fool horoscope first. Always saying how Addie's his good-luck piece and can't ever let her go. No use treating him like he's got any sense."

Will turned around and scrutinized Addie Adair, as if hoping to find someone who would finally listen to him without talking back. He sighed.

"Let me get this straight, Jonas. You nabbed Addie. Then you stashed her here with some half-baked scheme about setting her up as a headstone."

"So I didn't have all the details worked out beforehand." Jonas sounded defensive. "Had to act fast, William. Figured after the uproar was over I'd find a way to get Addie settled in that cemetery right. Then you brought your newspaper lady friend to Sid's Place. Started me to thinking. Maybe uproar was what I needed, after all. Make it a big hullabaloo, me taking Addie, and Sid might change his mind about what kind of luck she brings. Might want to get rid of her, once and for all."

"Why, that's a brilliant plan," Erin exclaimed, beaming at Jonas. "And it's bound to work. There's nothing like the power of the press."

"Lord, I don't believe I'm hearing any of this." Will dug a hand into his hair. "You're crazy as loons, the two of you."

Erin twisted the lens cap off her camera. "Jonas, stand over there next to Addie Adair. Put your hand on her shoulder, the way you had it before. Yes, that's good. All right, here we go." She focused and snapped the picture, the flash going off. A second later Will's fingers curled around the camera strap. He tugged Erin toward him, a menacing expression on his face.

"I won't let you exploit Jonas like this." His voice was low but steely.

Erin kept both hands clamped around her camera. She had visions of Will grabbing it and ripping out the film. She gazed at him steadily, refusing to back down.

"I'm going to write this story, Will. No one can stop me. Not even you."

Jonas cackled, patting Addie's cheek where the rosy paint of her complexion was peeling off. "We'll show this town a good time, girl. No more hiding and skulking around. Your picture belongs in the papers, that's the truth of it."

"You see, Will?" Erin asked. "This is what Jonas wants, too. You can't stop it from happening."

Will's hand tightened on the camera strap and he brought her face inches nearer to his. "You talk about ideals all the time, Lewis. You talk about making the world a better place to live. But when it comes right down to it, you have no compassion for one sick and frail old man."

"Ain't dead yet, William," Jonas interjected with asperity. "Still got some strength left. Could whip you at arm wrestling any day."

Will ignored him, all his attention centered on Erin. "You're a user, Lewis, exactly like your Uncle Ned. You talk about your grand visions, but in the end you just use people. That's what you're doing now with Jonas, so you'll have a story that sells newspapers."

Erin didn't flinch outwardly, but inside she recoiled from the contempt she saw in his eyes. He was wrong about her—all wrong! She wanted to write a story about two people who had loved each other. She wanted to write about an irascible old man who still carried that love in his soul. It would be a tribute to Jonas, not a dishonor. She tried one more time to make Will understand.

"Listen, this story really matters to me! It touches me in a personal way. I know I can make other people feel what I do for Jonas and Luisa. Sympathy, admiration...they won't blame Jonas for what he did, I can promise you that. Oh, Will, this is what journalism means to me. Can't you see? Finding a story that captures me, that speaks to my heart. I'll make it speak to everybody else's heart, too.''

"You give a good speech, Lewis. Heck, maybe you're even sincere about all this. But that doesn't change anything. You're still using Jonas for your own purposes.''

She couldn't seem to make him understand. How she wished he would really listen to her, really hear what she was trying to say. Earlier tonight he'd given her his tenderness. But it was gone now, replaced by scorn. It hurt deeply, knowing that he couldn't feel for her what Jonas had felt for Luisa all these years. But it only confirmed her wisdom in shielding herself from him . . . in keeping her emotions firmly under control when it came to Will Kendrick.

And she was very much in control when she stared coldly at him. She didn't betray any of the hurt.

"I'm going to print this story,'' she said, without faltering. "No matter what you say or do, Will, I'm going to print it.''

CHAPTER ELEVEN

A WEEK LATER MAGGIE KENDRICK catapulted into Erin's office. She was wearing a dramatic red dress that billowed all about her, with two matching red ribbons in her pile of hair. Her feet wobbled in high-heeled shoes that were also bright red. She looked like an exuberant Christmas candle, topped by the silvery-blond flame of her hair. Moving at runaway speed, she managed to land all in one piece—and right-side up—in the chair by Erin's desk. She waved some sheets of paper in the air, her lovely hazel eyes gyrating with excitement.

"Here it is!" she proclaimed. "My first 'Ask Maggie' column. I can't wait for you to read it, Erin. Did I tell you I got my nameplate today? Maggie S. Kendrick, just like we decided. In gold letters. And I really do believe I need new curtains in my office. I'll sew them myself. Something in a tangerine color, I think. That will inspire me when I'm working on my column. Any shade of orange has deep psychological impact, you know. Very deep." Maggie's eyes darted from side to side as if she was experiencing the psychological impact of orange this very minute.

Erin reached over and extracted the sheets of paper from Maggie's hand before this conversation became too convoluted. She smoothed out a letter printed forcefully on blue stationery with a border of plump yellow kittens frolicking at the bottom.

Dear Maggie,

I have a problem. My husband talks to his cats. All the time, Maggie. We're sitting there eating dinner and Fred has his head under the table, talking to the cats instead of me. Or else the damn cats are prancing around on top of the table. And that's not all, Maggie. Every one of my birthdays Fred buys me cat mugs, cat calendars or cat pot holders. One year it was a cat mobile. He hung it over the bed. I've just about had it with the cats, Maggie. Please advise.

Sincerely,
Jinxed in Jamesport

Maggie's reply was written in a wild script, with several words crossed out and a great deal of scribbling in the margin. Reading it was tough going, but Erin finally deciphered all of it.

Dear Jinxed,

I sense that your cat situation is reaching a crisis point. Desperate measures may be called for. Have you considered treating Fred's tabbies to a long weekend in a cat hotel? Once you are safely alone with Fred, present him with a romantic dinner by candlelight. Make sure you don't use the cat pot holders, however. The idea is to create a cat-free environment for Fred (vacuum up all hair balls beforehand). Hopefully Fred will discover there is life after catnip.

I must warn you, however, that many cat people cannot change. They will remain feline fanatics forever. If this is the case with Fred, you might consider buying a dog for yourself. Perhaps a large Labrador or a Doberman. At least your dinner conversations will be more lively.

Good luck,
Maggie

Erin tapped her fingers against the top of the desk. Maggie leaned toward her, eyes rotating anxiously.

"Well, what do you think? I've been working on it all afternoon."

"Um . . ." Erin was at a loss for words. She didn't know exactly *what* she thought of Maggie's column. She stacked some file folders together while she tried to come up with an opinion. "I believe you've taken a fresh approach," she said at last. "Yes, that's it. A fresh approach."

This seemed to satisfy Maggie completely. Her hair bobbed up and down a bit, red ribbons quivering. "I'm so glad you like it! That means we can get on to something else. Your own romantic problems, Erin."

Erin snapped a rubber band around one of the file folders. "I don't have any romantic problems."

"Oh, but you do, my dear." Maggie waved her hands, ruby nails gleaming in the late afternoon sun. "You and Will have a problem together. You were meant for each other—absolutely, no argument about it. But neither of you can seem to see that."

Erin felt herself flushing in agitation. The last thing she wanted to talk about right now was Will Kendrick. It was bad enough thinking about him all the time. But Maggie wouldn't give up. She scooted her chair closer to the desk, her eyes zeroing in on Erin. It was always disconcerting when Maggie's gaze found a resting place for a moment.

"Let me tell you, Will hasn't been at all himself lately. He's been snarling at everyone, thoroughly out of temper, the dear boy. I've never seen him more disagreeable." Maggie smiled as if delighted with Will's grouchy behavior. "He wouldn't be acting like this if it wasn't for you, Erin. No, indeed."

Erin rubbed her temples, trying to loosen up tense muscles. "It only goes to prove that Will and I don't belong anywhere near each other. I make him act like an enraged yak, and he makes me *feel* like an enraged yak. We're definitely not good for each other."

"Nonsense." Maggie's eyes sprang into motion again, as lively as two Ping-Pong balls. "You're a perfect couple. A match made in heaven. Dear Ned is probably sending his influence over both of you from beyond. Isn't that wonderful? He hasn't really left us at all."

Erin gave a pale smile. It certainly was true that the subject of Uncle Ned had caused no end of trouble between her and Will. "Maggie...I just don't think it's that simple. Will keeps telling me I'm too much like my uncle. And he wasn't exactly fond of Ned."

"Now, you mustn't listen to Will. Sometimes he concentrates a little too much on Ned's bad points instead of the good ones, that's all there is to it." Maggie bounced out of her chair. "I'm glad we have that settled! I'd better get back to work now. I've decided that I must include my recipe for bran muffins in my first column." She careened out of the room and down the hall to her own office.

Erin rubbed her temples with more vigor. She hadn't seen Will for two days, not since he'd come barging into her office with a scrawled sheet of ad copy for Kendrick's Boat Yard. She'd been surprised that he'd decided to advertise in the *Gazette,* after all—even agreeing to a full-page ad. No one else in Jamesport was willing to advertise in the newspaper yet, in spite of Erin's countless phone calls and visits to businesspeople after that unsatisfactory banquet. To have Will be the one person who came through for her... that really meant something. But he'd stalked out of her office before she could so much as thank him. And now she wanted to see him again. She wanted to be in his arms, to relearn the touch of his lips...

Confound it! What she really wanted was to slap him over the head with her first edition of the *Cape Cod Gazette.* She had to get busy and stop thinking about Will once and for all, or there wouldn't be any newspaper tomorrow. She pushed back her chair and stood up with renewed determination.

The rest of the afternoon passed in a flurry. She finished writing a tribute to Uncle Ned that would go on the second page, right next to Maggie's column. Meanwhile, national news stories streamed in from the wire service, rattling into life on the old Teletype receiver. Erin spent over an hour on the phone to some of her contacts in Boston, gleaning the latest information on a convening of environmentalists to discuss the problem of oil spills. While she was still on the phone, Lyle Ferris loped into her office. Lyle was her sixteen-year-old reporter/janitor/sports editor. He delivered his news copy onto her desk, then carefully rearranged his hair. This was something to watch: Lyle bending forward, then tossing his head back so his long sandy hair would sweep at just the right angle across his forehead. Afterwards he gave Erin a salute and loped out of her office again. Lyle was a boy of few words, and this characteristic carried over to his writing. Whatever he put down on paper was clean and spare. He had the makings of an excellent journalist, if only he'd give in to a little punctuation.

Erin jotted down a few more notes on her pad as she spoke into the telephone receiver. "All right, thanks. That ought to do it." She hung up and scanned Lyle's copy. Good, he'd wrapped up the story on the whale-watch tours. Now she cranked a fresh piece of paper into Uncle Ned's ancient typewriter and started thrashing out an article on the environmentalists' meeting. The keys were so stiff she had to bring a finger down on each one like a kamikaze pilot crashing in for a bombing. She decided to consider this a form of exercise. If she kept it up, she'd have the strongest fingers known to womankind. Not that she had much choice; she had no money to spare for new equipment.

It was dark outside before Erin made her way to the composing room. An update had come in over the wire service about the vice-president's Latin American tour, and Lyle had nosed out some more information on a house fire in Wellfleet. Now Erin dumped her pages of copy and her sketched mock-up of the completed newspaper onto one of the worktables. She couldn't afford to hire any more employees, which meant she had to juggle several different jobs herself. Grabbing a thick canvas apron from its peg on the wall, she tied it around her waist. The apron was smeared and smudged with ink after years of use. Erin felt good wearing it. With ease she fell into the habits she'd learned over her summers spent working with Ned. But the composing room seemed too empty without her uncle's presence, the overhead lights shining down garishly on the clutter of machinery.

At the keyboard of the Linotype, Erin began setting type for her story on Jonas and Luisa. Brass letter molds dropped out of their storage magazines and into the line assembler, announcing The True Identity of Addie Adair. Erin had rewritten the story a dozen times. She would have kept on rewriting and polishing, but the newspaper had to go to press. She'd tried so hard to portray the love between Jonas and Luisa. Had she succeeded at all?

"Hello, Erin." She heard Will's voice from the doorway. She started and turned toward him, her heart pounding. After two days of not seeing him, he looked more attractive than ever to her. He was wearing a faded khaki shirt that emphasized the tan on his arms. His sleeves were rolled up carelessly and one side of his collar was twisted under. Erin doubted that Will ever looked in the mirror after getting dressed. She liked that about him. She liked it a lot. But she wasn't going to let him know it, that was for sure.

"What are you doing here?" she demanded, wiping damp palms against her apron.

He came into the room and glanced around. "Maggie told me you were shorthanded. She said there was no way you were going to get this newspaper out by yourself. Besides, Lewis, you keep forgetting I have a vested interest in the *Gazette*. I'm supposed to be here."

"I have everything under control." She swiveled back to the keyboard and started working again. Faster and faster she pushed the machine to cast each line of letter mats into a slug of type. If she concentrated on this and nothing else, maybe Will would go away and leave her alone.

But he didn't leave. He stood right behind her. "Just tell me what to do. You need my help and you know it."

She didn't want to depend on him for anything. Her fingers accelerated still more on the keyboard. "Have you changed your mind about Jonas's story?" she asked. "Is that why you're so eager to help me?"

"Lord, no. I've been spending all my time trying to convince Jonas not to go public. He won't listen, as usual. And in the end I have to respect his wishes. This is what he wants, no matter how stupid I think it is."

"You're certainly magnanimous." She kept her voice stiff. "But you can go home now. I don't want you here. As long as you're respecting other people's wishes, you might as well comply with mine."

"Dammit, Erin, let's just get the blasted newspaper out. Then Maggie'll be happy, Jonas'll be happy, you'll be happy. Everyone will be overjoyed except for me!"

She hesitated. His presence was compelling. Even though he took such a sour view of her newspaper, the composing room no longer felt lonely. After another minute she nodded.

"All right," she said, businesslike. "Why don't you start by rounding up all the chases for me. That means the page forms—I see a few over there. Make sure they're empty of any old type."

Erin was surprised at how well she and Will worked together. He did get a mutinous expression on his face every time she rapped out instructions at him, but he followed them quickly and efficiently. It reminded her of that day on the *Marianna,* when she'd followed *his* instructions about sailing. Once again she and Will were sharing a camaraderie, in spite of all the strain between them.

They didn't speak much as the hours sped by. Erin was dismayed whenever she glanced at her watch and saw how much time had passed. She admitted grudgingly to herself that without Will's help the newspaper would've been out late. She hated being so shorthanded, but until the *Gazette* started to earn some money she couldn't afford to hire more workers.

The newspaper building was hot and stuffy in the summer night. Patches of sweat had formed on Will's back and under his arms. Erin watched him as he bent over to scan yet another galley proof for errors. She drew the back of her hand across her forehead, gazing at the way Will's muscles flexed under his sweat-dampened shirt as he paused to stretch.

He glanced over at her. "Tired?" he asked. Erin blinked and hurried back to the Linotype. She wished she could step under a stream of water to cool her flushed body.

"I'm fine," she said. "Just fine."

At last they were ready to move into the press-room. Here Erin was nervous, praying that the cross-tempered press wouldn't break down. There was one horrible moment when the machine refused to start. But then it growled into life. Gradually it picked up speed, causing a racket like ten soreheaded monsters who didn't want to get out of bed.

Erin grinned at Will, poking her thumb into the air in a gesture of victory. He grinned back, apparently his own temper quite improved. After that only a few minor hitches occurred as they worked together.

"Web's not tight enough!" Erin shouted.

"Got it," Will yelled back over the roar of the press.

"More ink," Erin called. Then, a little later, "No, that's too much!"

Will continued to man the ink fountains under her direction. Erin pushed a damp curl back from her cheek. She took a deep whiff of air, breathing in the smells of ink and machine oil and newsprint paper. How she loved these odors!

A copy of the *Gazette* was coming off the folder. She snatched it up to check the page numbers and scan the headlines. There on the front page was the photograph of Jonas, his hand clamped on Addie Adair, his posture defiant in spite of the stoop of his shoulders. And there was Erin's story about him. It was a reality at last . . . the rebirth of the *Cape Cod Gazette*. A sense of pride and happiness filled her, sweeping away any trace of weariness.

Will took the newspaper from her and frowned at it. His genial mood seemed to have vanished, replaced once again by disgust. He didn't even bother to read the paper—just tossed it down onto a table.

"You did it," he said. "You put Jonas out there where he's going to be vulnerable and at everyone's mercy."

It was difficult to hear him over the noise of the machine. Erin marched up closer to him.

"Don't ruin this moment for me, Will!" she yelled. "I've been dreaming about it for a long time now. Just leave it alone!"

He gripped her arms and brought his face down next to hers. He bellowed into her ear. "I'm going to say my piece, Lewis. If it'd been up to me and no one else, the *Cape Cod Gazette* never would've seen the light of day again. I don't agree with anything you're doing here. It bugs the heck out of me how you can spout off about your ideals, then turn around and exploit someone like Jonas. I can't believe I almost fell for you. I almost let something happen between us."

She glared at him. "I'd never get involved with you!" she shouted over all the racket of the press. "I want a man who respects what I do, what I believe."

He laughed harshly. "What you want is someone who'll pat you on the back and tell you how noble you are. You wouldn't get that from me. I'd give you something real and basic instead. I might even give you love, Erin. But that's what you're afraid of, isn't it? Real emotion."

"Damn you, Will Kendrick." Her voice was growing hoarse, but she ignored the ache in her throat. "Just get the hell out of here. And stay the hell out of my life!"

"It's too bad you're afraid to feel, Erin." His voice was low now, and she had to strain to hear it. "You're going to stumble through the rest of your life searching for the ideal man, but you'll never find him. And secretly you'll be relieved about that because you're so afraid to risk love. Good luck hiding from life.'' His gaze traveled over her face, and for a second his dark eyes seemed to hold a tenderness for her. But then his features tensed into hardness again.

"Goodbye, Erin," he said. The words had an unmistakable finality. He let go of her and strode from the room. Erin was left alone with the clatter and roar of the old printing press. She reached out one ink-stained hand as if to call Will back to her.

But it was too late. He was gone.

CHAPTER TWELVE

ERIN STABBED HER PENCIL into one of the many nicks on her desk. "...eighty-eight, eighty-seven, eighty-six..." she muttered, trying to cool her temper. She'd been stewing ever since her confrontation with Will last night. So he thought she was afraid of real emotions. She was experiencing some genuine emotions this very instant. Anger, resentment, bitterness! She'd had enough of Will's ridicule, his contempt for her uncle and everything she believed in. "...sixty-one, sixty, fifty-nine...take that, Will Kendrick!" She gouged at another nick in the desk, then threw down her pencil in exasperation. Surely she could think about something else besides Will. She was finished with him. Everything was over between the two of them before it had even started. That was exactly the way she wanted it!

Erin flipped through her dog-eared phone book, still muttering various curses and complaints under her breath. She grabbed up the telephone receiver and dialed a number. She had to fight her way through two secretaries, but finally she was on the line to Roger Paxton.

"Good morning, Roger," she said, interjecting a forced cheerfulness into her voice. "Just wondering if you'd read today's edition of the *Cape Cod Gazette*."

"Yes, I have," he responded in his courtly manner. Erin pictured his boxer's face, and had trouble matching it with his elegant, cultivated voice. "As a matter of fact," he went on, "your overzealous paperboy nearly took out the front window of my house this morning."

Erin winced. Maybe she'd given her sixteen-year-old assistant one too many jobs to do by making him into a paperboy. "Anyway, Roger, I wondered what you thought of the *Gazette*."

"It was interesting," came his noncommittal reply.

Erin's fingers tightened on the receiver. "You have to admit that the *Gazette* will attract some attention now. People are going to start reading it."

"Perhaps. But it's too early to make predictions of any kind."

Erin resisted the urge to slam the receiver down in his ear. "All I'm asking from you is an appointment so we can discuss advertising possibilities. Surely it won't hurt you to hear me out."

"Shall we make it over dinner? That is, unless you're still seeing Kendrick."

Erin sat up straight in her battered leather chair. "Now, listen here, Roger. I am not involved with Will Kendrick. I have never been involved with Will Kendrick. I wouldn't be involved with Will Kendrick if you paid me a million dollars!"

"I see. You're that serious about him." Roger's voice was regretful. "I don't waste energy pursuing either a woman or a business deal when returns aren't likely."

"Roger—"

"Tell you what, Erin. You have proved something to me today, I'll grant you that. You're stubborn and a damn good journalist. Maybe it wouldn't be such a bad idea for me to advertise in your newspaper—we'll see. Drop by my office tomorrow at ten-thirty and I'll give you a few minutes." He hung up as if eager to be on his way to more profitable ventures.

Erin slowly lowered her own telephone receiver. She'd achieved an appointment with Roger Paxton. That was something—a beginning. She knew she could convince him to advertise in the *Gazette!* And after that, surely other advertisers would follow. So why wasn't she happy? She deserved to be happy, damn it.

Several calls came in for 'Ask Maggie.' Whenever Erin passed through the hall, she'd hear Maggie talking earnestly on the telephone in her office. The snatches of conversation were intriguing and sometimes a bit disturbing: "Yes, dear, I really think you ought to shop around for a new boyfriend. Besides, you're only forty-five. Why tie yourself down?" And then, later: "No, I could swear it's three cups of rolled oats. Why don't you try the recipe again and call me back? Everyone loves my bran muffins, you know."

Erin hovered outside Maggie's office. She was about to slip away when Maggie hung up the phone and saw her.

"Isn't all this wonderful, Erin?" she exclaimed, beckoning with a flash of red fingernails. "If only Ned was here to see us. But I *do* believe he's watching from somewhere. I'm sure he's very pleased with us."

Erin came into the room and sank into a chair across from the desk. She stared gloomily at the nameplate which spelled out "Maggie S. Kendrick" in gold letters. "I wish I could believe Uncle Ned would be happy. But I'm not sure about anything anymore. Not about Ned. Certainly not about Will..." Erin stopped, dismayed at how easy it was to confide in the older woman.

Maggie bounced up and down a little in her chair, the silvery-blond curls piled on her head jiggling in rhythm. Today she was swathed in billows and billows of bright orange cloth. They didn't look structured enough to be called a dress. Perhaps Maggie had bought the material to make curtains for her office, then decided she'd rather wear it instead. The color was certainly a striking contrast to her red fingernails.

"Now, Erin, dear, we really must do something about you and Will. This can't go on." Maggie's gaze darted about as if she was searching the room for possible solutions.

Erin let out an explosive sigh. "There's nothing to be done! The best thing I can do is forget about him. He's made me doubt everything I ever believed in. Even Uncle Ned. Oh, Maggie—"

"Don't ever stop believing in Ned." Maggie's voice was forceful, and her eyes swiveled back and forth with greater energy. "Erin, your uncle had plenty of faults, I'm not denying that. He liked a few too many women, he was impractical and an atrocious businessman. And maybe that's all Will could see—those faults. But you and I know the good things. Ned made us feel happy. He helped us discover our visions! Does anything else really matter?''

Erin had always idolized her uncle, always believed he was perfect. Now even Maggie was telling her that Ned had possessed faults. Perhaps she finally had to accept that, along with all her good memories of him. She had loved Ned, but he hadn't been an ideal man. Was she relieved or disappointed to finally realize that? She just didn't know!

Maggie was watching her with that disconcerting shrewdness. ''Erin, dear, you're too fidgety to sit here talking to me. You'd better run down to the boat yard and see what's happening. If you're going to do a follow-up story on Jonas and Addie Adair, you need to get started right away.''

''Maggie, you sure seem to like giving out advice,'' Erin said ruefully.

''Of course! That's my new job, isn't it?'' Maggie's lovely hazel eyes snapped wildly about. ''And right now it's your job to follow my advice.''

Maggie was implacable. A few moments later Erin found herself stalking down Main Street, her straw hat jammed onto her head. Actually, she *did* have a few things to say to Will Kendrick. She couldn't let him get away with his cavalier treatment of her. Last night he'd accused her of being a coward, and that rankled more than anything.

It was a glorious morning, with a sky as clear and blue as an Easter-egg shell. Erin had never known fine weather to make her grumpy, but it was happening today. Then she saw a woman sitting at one of the tables of an outdoor cafe. . . a copy of the *Cape Cod Gazette* held up in front of her. That did a lot to improve Erin's disposition—seeing someone read her newspaper.

Erin arrived at the boat yard, out of breath because she'd jogged the last few blocks. She found Jonas hunched at the counter of the tackle shop, thumbing through one of his sports magazines. He looked Erin over with his rheumy gaze. Then, as if he found her unworthy of further perusal, he went back to an article on sumo wrestling.

"So what's been happening?" she asked. "What about Captain Sid—has he been down to talk to you yet?"

"Don't get yourself in a tizzy fit. Life goes on, missie, even when you're not around to report it."

Erin pushed one of her wild red curls out of her face. "Jonas, sometimes your charm overwhelms me. It really does."

He gave his cackle of a laugh. "'Course, Sid was already here, first thing this morning. Stinging mad like a jellyfish, he was. Some other folks came along, too. Ends up everybody tells him Addie's bad luck now till she finds her way to the cemetery. No sense in messing with the dead. That's what I told Sid, and he starts looking real worried." Jonas cackled again, the sound like rusty nails scraping over wood.

"Sid starts looking over his shoulder like he sees vampires. Didn't take too much to convince him after that. Turns out Sid's going to lead a procession to the cemetery with Addie Adair, day after tomorrow. Figures it'll be good luck if he plays his harmonica. Going to make a speech, too, the old goat." Jonas gave a malevolent grin and turned a page of his magazine.

"So we did it! Having the story in the newspaper worked. You and me, Jonas, we did it."

"Leave me be, missie. Told you everything already. What you really want is to go pester William. He's out in the work building. Sprucing up a boat." Jonas yawned, exposing every one of his yellowed teeth. He went on reading about sumo wrestlers.

Erin strode outside to the large barn-like building across from the tackle shop. Its big double doors were flung wide, but even so daylight had trouble penetrating the dimness inside. The single bare bulb hanging from the rafters of the high ceiling didn't do much to dispel the shadows, either. Erin stood on the threshold, peering about for Will.

After a moment Duffy materialized from a dark corner, trotting up to Erin with his tongue hanging out in a friendly way. She leaned down to pet his scraggly ears, then followed him into the immense gloom of the place. Her feet scuffed over sawdust as she walked.

A sailboat was propped up by a wooden framework at the far end of the building, and this was where Duffy led her. Light glimmered from behind the boat, where the tapping of a hammer could be heard. After a pause the light shifted and then Will appeared, holding up an old-fashioned lantern as he watched Erin's approach.

She stopped a few feet away from him. "Hello, Will," she said in a calm voice.

"Hello, Erin." His own voice was equally calm. He put the lantern on top of some crates and went on watching her. Darn, it made her jittery to face that cool, assessing gaze of his. But no matter what Will

Kendrick said about her, she wasn't a coward. She tilted her chin and stared back defiantly at him.

"I came to tell you something. Tomorrow I have an appointment with Roger Paxton. Things are starting to look very promising for the *Gazette*. It shouldn't be all that long before I begin making payments to Maggie."

"Is this one of those dinner appointments with Paxton? Something nice and cozy between the two of you?"

Will sounded downright jealous. Erin frowned at him. "Not that it's any business of yours, but Roger still thinks you and I are involved somehow. He's decided I'm not worth the effort of pursuing, as long as you're hanging around."

"Good."

"You made it pretty clear last night you wouldn't be hanging around me any longer," she pointed out.

"Hell." He ran a hand through his hair until it looked as unruly as Duffy's. "Listen, Lewis, I have something to say to you."

"Forget it. You said more than enough to me last night."

"Just hear me out, will you?" He began to pace back and forth, hands stuffed into the pockets of his jeans. "I read your story about Jonas. Okay, I read it a couple of times. All right, so I read the blasted thing until I practically had it memorized. It was...effective. I'll say that for you, Lewis. You're an effective writer. And you've proved that you can turn the *Cape Cod Gazette* into a real newspaper."

"Wait a minute. Is this actually praise I hear coming from your mouth? Praise for me? I must be imagining things."

"You're not making this any easier," Will growled. "I still think your ideas about life are way too high-flown. But the way you told that story about Jonas and Luisa...you talked about a world where love really can endure. Heck, you made me envy a world like that." Will sounded very grouchy now. He came over to her and scowled, looking like an irritated bear that had just lumbered out of its cave. "Erin, you drive me crazy. I figure you always will drive me crazy. There's only one way for you to put me out of my misery. You'll have to marry me. No discussion—that's it. You have to marry me."

Her heart started thudding at a most alarming tempo. She folded her arms across her chest. "I can't believe you used the *M* word. But it's bad enough having a business deal with you! If we got married, we'd both end up crazy."

"Look, I'll clean up the dirty socks in my house. Does that make you happy? But no groomer is coming anywhere near McDuff. Got that?"

She tried to keep a solemn expression on her face. "I don't know, Will. Seems to me you're asking for a lot of trouble here. If I move into your house, next thing you know I might be sneaking Duffy out in the middle of the night—leading him straight to the scissors."

"You're right. What am I letting myself in for?" he grumbled. "There's no controlling you, Lewis. Look at you." He took her hand in his and gazed down at it. "You're going to run around the rest of your life with newspaper ink all over your fingers, chasing dreams and visions about some grand kind of world. And there's not a thing I can do to stop you. After reading your story, I don't even know if I want to stop you anymore. That's what really has me worried.'' He traced his finger ever so gently over her palm, sending a shiver of delight all through her.

Erin couldn't restrain a grin any longer. Will Kendrick was the most stubborn, domineering, mule-headed man she'd ever known. He found it extremely difficult to admit when he was wrong about something, or to back down once he'd taken a stand. He was not perfect by any standard; he didn't live up to some idealized vision in her head. And as far as she was concerned, that was wonderful. She flung her arms around him and hung on to his solid strength for all she was worth.

''I love you, Will,'' she said against his rumpled shirt. ''I love everything about you. I love knowing it's probably been ten years since you bought any new clothes. I love you defending and protecting Maggie, even when she's sneaking around behind your back to get her own way. I love to watch you tie knots and to hear you singing off-key in Portuguese when you're hoisting a sail. Basically, I love you.''

His own arms came around her and she heard laughter rumbling deep in his chest.

''Matchstick, it's about time you said that to me.''

She planted her hands flat on his chest. ''I knew I never should have told you about that nickname!'' she exclaimed. ''I knew someday you'd use it against me.''

''You have to admit it fits you. After all, you do have a mighty quick temper to go with this pretty red mane of yours.'' He buried his hands in the masses of her hair, his eyes dark with tenderness and desire. ''Don't worry, though, Erin. The secret of Matchstick will always be safe with me. You can trust me on that. You do trust me, don't you?'' His voice was husky now.

She took a shaky breath. Admitting she loved Will was like saying yes to a tidal wave of emotion. Maybe it would always be scary, the fact that she could feel love this strong. But for too many years now she'd been stifling her capacity for intense emotion, hiding behind her idealized version of Uncle Ned. And yet, that had actually been a betrayal of Ned and what he stood for. Hadn't he always told her to go out and live life to its fullest? And Will had taught her that her life would be lonely and empty if she didn't take the risk of loving him.

''Yes, I trust you,'' she answered, running her hands over the worn cloth of his shirt. ''Will, you were right. All along I've been trying to protect myself from getting hurt. That was easy enough until you came along. I kept trying to convince myself that you were too complacent, that you didn't want to change the world the way you should. But what you have is really important. Caring about people like Maggie and Jonas...''

She couldn't talk anymore after that because Will took her face between his hands and kissed her. He tasted fresh and salty, like the ocean itself. His kiss was so thorough and complete that her hat soon went tumbling down her back, unheeded.

After a very long moment Will and Erin broke apart, both of them out of breath.

"Lord, sweetheart, what you do to me." Will's voice was unsteady. "But I need to show you something." He picked up his lantern to illuminate the sailboat. The boat had simple, graceful lines much like those of the *Marianna*. It was made of amber-colored wood that gleamed in the lantern light. And spelled out in fresh white paint over the satiny grain of the wood was the name "Erin Lee."

"I like the sound of that," Will said in a satisfied tone. "I like to think of you and me standing together in the lee of the wind, keeping each other warm. So naturally that's what I had to name this tub. I've been working on her for years, but I never did know what to call her until now."

Joy swept through Erin like a clean fresh breeze straight from Cape Cod Bay. "A whole boat, named after me?"

"You know what my grandfather always said. A man has to name a boat after a woman to prove how much he loves her. I do love you, Erin. I came to the boat yard last night, looking for a way to work out the frustrations I was feeling because of you. And all I could think of was hauling out the paint can and christening this boat with your name."

He drew her back into his arms. "Erin, I love you," he repeated, murmuring the words against her cheek. "I think I could get used to saying that. Kind of grows on you after a while."

She linked her hands together behind his neck, relishing the silkiness of his hair under her fingers. "You can say those words all you like," she declared. "Especially when we're out sailing on the *Marianna*.

Or the *Erin Lee*. Oh, Will, I want to go sailing with you, forever and ever.''

''Hey, don't forget you have a newspaper to run. The Kendricks have a lot invested in that *Cape Cod Gazette* of yours.''

''Somehow we'll fit it all in, all the adventures we're going to share together.'' She moved closer into the circle of his arms. Duffy licked her ankle and then settled down contentedly beside her to gnaw on her hat. Erin was right where she belonged, surrounded by the Kendrick clan. She didn't need anything else, not anything at all.

At last she'd reached love's harbor.

HARLEQUIN
Romance®

**This November,
travel to England with
Harlequin Romance
FIRST CLASS title #3159,
AN ANSWER FROM THE HEART
by Claudia Jameson**

It was unsettling enough that the company she worked for
was being taken over, but Maxine was appalled at the
prospect of having Kurt Raynor as her new boss. She was
quite content with things the way they were, even if the
arrogant, dynamic Mr. Raynor had other ideas and was
expecting her to be there whenever he whistled. However
Maxine wasn't about to hand in her notice yet; Kurt had
offered her a challenge and she was going to rise to it—after
all, he wasn't asking her to change her whole life . . . was
he?

HARLEQUIN
Romance

A Christmas tradition...

Imagine spending Christmas in New Orleans with a blind stranger and his aged guide dog—when you're supposed to be there on your honeymoon!
#3163 Every Kind of Heaven
by Bethany Campbell

Imagine spending Christmas with a man you once "married"—in a mock ceremony at the age of eight!
#3166 The Forgetful Bride
by Debbie Macomber

Available in December 1991, wherever Harlequin books are sold.

"INDULGE A LITTLE" SWEEPSTAKES

HERE'S HOW THE SWEEPSTAKES WORKS

NO PURCHASE NECESSARY

To enter each drawing, complete the appropriate Official Entry Form or a 3" by 5" index card by hand-printing your name, address and phone number and the trip destination that the entry is being submitted for (i.e., Walt Disney World Vacation Drawing, etc.) and mailing it to: Indulge '91 Subscribers-Only Sweepstakes, P.O. Box 1397, Buffalo, New York 14269-1397.

No responsibility is assumed for lost, late or misdirected mail. Entries must be sent separately with first class postage affixed, and be received by: 9/30/91 for the Walt Disney World Vacation Drawing, 10/31/91 for the Alaskan Cruise Drawing and 11/30/91 for the Hawaiian Vacation Drawing. Sweepstakes is open to residents of the U.S. and Canada, 21 years of age or older as of 11/7/91.

For complete rules, send a self-addressed, stamped (WA residents need not affix return postage) envelope to: Indulge '91 Subscribers-Only Sweepstakes Rules, P.O. Box 4005, Blair, NE 68009.

© 1991 HARLEQUIN ENTERPRISES LTD.   DIR-RL

"INDULGE A LITTLE" SWEEPSTAKES

HERE'S HOW THE SWEEPSTAKES WORKS

NO PURCHASE NECESSARY

To enter each drawing, complete the appropriate Official Entry Form or a 3" by 5" index card by hand-printing your name, address and phone number and the trip destination that the entry is being submitted for (i.e., Walt Disney World Vacation Drawing, etc.) and mailing it to: Indulge '91 Subscribers-Only Sweepstakes, P.O. Box 1397, Buffalo, New York 14269-1397.

No responsibility is assumed for lost, late or misdirected mail. Entries must be sent separately with first class postage affixed, and be received by: 9/30/91 for the Walt Disney World Vacation Drawing, 10/31/91 for the Alaskan Cruise Drawing and 11/30/91 for the Hawaiian Vacation Drawing. Sweepstakes is open to residents of the U.S. and Canada, 21 years of age or older as of 11/7/91.

For complete rules, send a self-addressed, stamped (WA residents need not affix return postage) envelope to: Indulge '91 Subscribers-Only Sweepstakes Rules, P.O. Box 4005, Blair, NE 68009.

© 1991 HARLEQUIN ENTERPRISES LTD.   DIR-RL

INDULGE A LITTLE—WIN A LOT!

Summer of '91 Subscribers-Only Sweepstakes

OFFICIAL ENTRY FORM

This entry must be received by: Sept. 30, 1991
This month's winner will be notified by: Oct. 7, 1991
Trip must be taken between: Nov. 7, 1991—Nov. 7, 1992

YES, I want to win the Walt Disney World® vacation for two. I understand the prize includes round-trip airfare, first-class hotel and pocket money as revealed on the "wallet" scratch-off card.

Name _____

Address_____ Apt. _____

City _____

State/Prov. _____ Zip/Postal Code _____

Daytime phone number _____
(Area Code)

Return entries with invoice in envelope provided. Each book in this shipment has two entry coupons—and the more coupons you enter, the better your chances of winning!

© 1991 HARLEQUIN ENTERPRISES LTD.   CPS-M1

INDULGE A LITTLE—WIN A LOT!

Summer of '91 Subscribers-Only Sweepstakes

OFFICIAL ENTRY FORM

This entry must be received by: Sept. 30, 1991
This month's winner will be notified by: Oct. 7, 1991
Trip must be taken between: Nov. 7, 1991—Nov. 7, 1992

YES, I want to win the Walt Disney World® vacation for two. I understand the prize includes round-trip airfare, first-class hotel and pocket money as revealed on the "wallet" scratch-off card.

Name _____

Address_____ Apt. _____

City _____

State/Prov. _____ Zip/Postal Code _____

Daytime phone number _____
(Area Code)

Return entries with invoice in envelope provided. Each book in this shipment has two entry coupons—and the more coupons you enter, the better your chances of winning!

© 1991 HARLEQUIN ENTERPRISES LTD.   CPS-M1